keep sweet

michele dominguez greene

Simon Pulse
New York   London   Toronto   Sydney

SIMON PULSE

An imprint of Simon & Schuster Children's Publishing Division
1230 Avenue of the Americas, New York, NY 10020
First Simon Pulse paperback edition March 2011
Copyright © 2010 by Michele Dominguez Greene
All rights reserved, including the right of reproduction in whole or in part in any form.
SIMON PULSE and colophon are registered trademarks of Simon & Schuster, Inc.
Also available in a Simon Pulse hardcover edition.
For information about special discounts for bulk purchases,
please contact Simon & Schuster Special Sales at 1-866-506-1949
or business@simonandschuster.com.
The Simon & Schuster Speakers Bureau can bring authors to your live event.
For more information or to book an event contact
the Simon & Schuster Speakers Bureau at 1-866-248-3049
or visit our website at www.simonspeakers.com.
Designed by Mike Rosamilia
The text of this book was set in Berling.
Manufactured in the United States of America
2 4 6 8 10 9 7 5 3 1
The Library of Congress has cataloged the hardcover edition as follows:
Greene, Michele, 1962–
Keep sweet / by Michele Dominguez Greene. — 1st Simon Pulse hardcover ed.
p. cm.
Summary: Alva, not quite fifteen, is content with the strict rules
that define her life in Pineridge, the walled community where she lives
with her father, his seven wives, and her twenty-nine siblings until
she is caught giving her long-time crush an innocent first kiss
and forced to marry a violent, fifty-year-old man.
ISBN 978-1-4169-8681-2 (hc)
[1. Coming of age—Fiction. 2. Fundamentalist Church of Jesus Christ
of Latter Day Saints—Fiction. 3. Mormons—Fiction. 4. Polygamy—Fiction.]
I. Title.
PZ7.G84243Ke 2010
[Fic]—dc22
2009041827
ISBN 978-1-4424-0977-4 (pbk)
ISBN 978-1-4391-5746-6 (eBook)

For my grandmother,
Tennessee Greene

prologue

"Alva Jane, meet me behind the barn before dark,
I have something important to tell you. . . ."

I CLOSED MY EYES AT THE MEMORY OF JOSEPH JOHN'S
face, flushed with excitement as he whispered those words to
me—the words that changed my life forever. Beside the barn
washed white by the sun, Joseph John had taken my hand and
said the words I had been waiting to hear. His father had agreed
to our marriage; he planned to speak to my father and the
prophet that very evening.

I knew I shouldn't do it, that it was wrong, but I felt a
rush of such excitement and joy that I couldn't help it: I kissed
him quickly, my lips brushing lightly over his, feeling their soft-
ness and searching as he leaned in to me. And then came Sister
Cora's voice and a rough hand on my collar. I lost my balance
and fell headlong into the nightmare I am living now.

One kiss brought me here, locked in this pitch-black root

cellar beneath the barn. I shivered; the evening temperature always drops in the desert. I heard the scurrying of rats overhead and moved away from the corner where I had been crouching. I was unable to lean or lie down, my legs felt stiff, my knees raw. I could feel the welts on my legs and back oozing blood. The sacred undergarments beneath my cotton dress stuck to the open wounds; each movement brought a stinging pain.

I closed my eyes to block out the vision of Joseph John being forced into Tom Pruitt's truck, the men pinning his arms behind him. And then my own father, Eldon Ray, in the back stall of the barn, wielding his belt, swinging it overhead and bringing it down upon my back. . . . My mother holding my wrists in a strong grip, looking at me with eyes shining bright and metallic. Was she suffering with me . . . or was she satisfied? Whatever she felt, she did nothing to stop my pain, even when I cried out to her.

Somewhere in the midnight silence, I heard the wild, frenzied cries of the coyotes as they closed in on their prey. The insane yipping and howling echoed off the red rocks and desolate plains of the Utah desert. My heart beat faster and the blood rushed to my head. I knew how the prey felt in that terrible moment: trapped, helpless. I lay on my stomach, pressing my face against the cool dirt floor, letting exhaustion take over. I felt something scurry over my leg but I did not bother to shake it off. *Perhaps I will sleep and never wake up; perhaps God will deliver me from the life that lies before me . . . or restore me to the life I knew just a few months earlier. . . .*

CHAPTER ONE

SISTER EMILY RANG A LARGE COWBELL, CALLING THE children of the Pineridge compound to class in the Zion Academy. From the kitchen window I could see the others running to the schoolhouse in the early morning heat, the air already crisp and dry. I untied my apron, shaking off the flour that covered it, and felt my eyelashes, heavy from the flecks of sugar caught in the tips. I'd risen before dawn, as usual, to help my mother make the loaves of bread for the family.

Together we make fourteen loaves each day—fourteen loaves of bread for the twenty-nine children and seven wives of my father, Eldon Ray Merrill, the sword and shield of the prophet. The muscles in my arms felt sore but they were getting stronger each day with the heavy kneading and shaping of the dough, which had been slow to rise that morning. I needed to hurry or I would be late to school.

As I ran to join the other girls, Lee Beth Pruitt called out to me. "Alva Jane, do you have the answers to the scripture quiz from last week?"

Lee Beth couldn't remember scripture to save her life and was always asking me for the answers to avoid a knuckle rap from Sister Emily's ever-ready ruler. I knew sharing the answers was cheating but I felt sorry for Lee Beth, so tall and awkward in her ill-fitting dresses handed down from her seven older sisters. By the time the shoes got to Lee Beth they looked about ready for the scrap heap. It didn't help things that besides being so gawky, she had a lazy eye that wandered off in its own direction whenever it pleased. The Lord hands out trials to all of us, and Lee Beth certainly had her share of them. I reached into my notebook and took out the homework, passing it to Lee Beth under the disapproving fish eye of Wendy Callers.

"One day you're going to get in trouble for that, Alva. Even if Sister Emily doesn't know you gave her the answers, the Lord will. And how will Lee Beth raise up her children right without memorizing scripture?" Wendy's voice was high and nasal and as usual, she was sticking her nose into everyone else's business.

I didn't respond, turning instead to catch the eye of my father, Eldon Ray, who was working to repair a rain gutter on the side of our house. He waved, a smile lighting up his handsome face.

"Have a good day, Gumdrop!" he called out, using my pet name.

I knew I was his favorite daughter, the most like my mother, who was his favorite wife. When I was younger, he would always bring me back a special sweet treat when he traveled into the city. It was usually a bag of spiced gumdrops. Even now that was I was almost grown, he still brought me something from time to time. Watching him as I walked by, I felt a rush of pride. My father was tall and broad shouldered, still fit at fifty-five. He hadn't gone fat around the middle or lost his thick wavy hair like so many of the other men in Pineridge. And he truly was a pillar of the community, sitting on the Priesthood Council and helping the prophet enforce the codes, rules, and requirements.

Here in Pineridge, people live right and proper, according to the scriptures of the Fundamentalist Latter Day Saints. We are God's chosen people, the upholders of the true faith. Outside our compound, the world is a dangerous place, but inside, everyone is safe and secure under the absolute power and wisdom of the prophet, Uncle Kenton Barton.

Two years earlier, Uncle Kenton had a revelation that my father was to sell his successful irrigation business to one of Uncle Kenton's brothers in Salt Lake, and although Daddy obeyed, I knew it was hard on him to become an employee in the company his own father had started. There wasn't as much money now as there had been before and Daddy had to travel quite a bit to oversee the building of the new FLDS community in Arizona, but those were sacrifices my father was glad to make to fulfill the prophet's revelations. He was an example of devotion and service and it made our whole family proud.

I waved back to Daddy and walked with the other girls past the large, lodge-style houses of the other prominent families in the community: the Bartons, the Jaynes, the Raynards. All of our houses were located close to the center of town and the main temple, whereas the lesser families lived closer to the business district, where we had all kinds of stores and our own police and fire departments. As we approached the Zion Academy I looked up to see the gold statue of the angel Moroni high atop the main temple and I felt the comfort of knowing that God's eye was upon our community.

Stepping into the schoolhouse, I followed Lee Beth into the girls' classroom and searched for a seat out of the line of sight of the teacher. Sister Emily, my father's second wife, has been teaching the classes since I was a little girl, and she is known for her short temper and free hand with punishment. Sister Emily has only four children and has never been one of my father's favorites. Daddy only married her to gain influence with her powerful family—at least that's what my mother says. She's told me the story many times.

At twenty-three my father had been a new arrival to the Brotherhood, fresh from college, eager to prove himself to the then prophet, Owen Barton, and to the Lord. He had suffered the loss of his parents, who were mainstream Mormons, in a terrible car crash and had inherited valuable real estate in Salt Lake, which he promptly signed over to the Brotherhood. The irrigation company that his father had built was thriving; he was definitely an asset to be valued. He took Uncle Owen's pretty, big-boned fifteen-year-old daughter, Cora, as a wife. He knew that by also marrying skinny, cross-eyed Emily, Cora's younger sister, he would curry even more favor with the prophet and be on track to the celestial kingdom when he died. After Daddy's marriage to the sisters, Uncle Owen took him under his wing. My father's fortunes had risen quickly and now he sat on the Priesthood Council deciding the fate of the community. He became the trusted confidant of Uncle Kenton, who had inherited the divine priesthood head from his father.

My mother, Maureen, is Daddy's fourth wife and has been his favorite since he brought her home as a fourteen-year-old bride. People say that I look very much like her, which is quite flattering since she is widely considered a beauty. We have the same wide smile and freckles, the same eyes as green as a leaf on a tree. Her hair is true red while mine is what they call strawberry blond. And although we wear ankle-length, long-sleeve dresses to cover our bodies in modesty, my mother has a womanly shape, made for childbearing. I hope one day to inherit that from her, since right now I am all arms and legs and gangly as a boy, even though I am nearly fifteen.

My mother makes pleasing her husband and keeping the covenants the foundation of her life, and with twelve children, she has done her best to honor the prophet's expectation that a woman give birth to a baby every year after marriage. As a result, even as a fourth wife she has the privilege of living with her children in the main house with Sister Cora and her family.

Our dining room is not big enough to hold the entire family of seven wives and all their children, so at Sunday dinner, we eat in shifts. Daddy had intended to keep adding on to the house but after he sold the irrigation business, there was never enough money to follow through—which is just fine with me since the house is crowded enough already. Sister Emily and her nine-year-old son, Thomas, live in two rooms on the first floor, next to the storage space. There are no windows but at least they are part of the main house, not like the trailers out back where the four other wives live with their children.

My siblings and I share a suite of three rooms upstairs with our mother. The boys have their own sleeping quarters, of course. My four younger sisters all share a room, which leaves Olive, Laura Jean, and me to share the large front room with our mother. As the first wife, Sister Cora has four rooms upstairs even though she doesn't need them, with only three of her six children still living at home.

I once complained to Mama that it's unfair that Sister Cora should have a private bedroom to share with Daddy, as well as her own sewing room, when Mama has contributed more children to what will be his heavenly kingdom. But Mama told me that it is not the number of rooms in the house that counts, it is the desire in our father's heart, and of that, Mama has the lion's share.

Mama's favor with Daddy sometimes makes the other wives resentful and jealous, especially Sister Cora, who is now forty-five and no longer able to be a vessel worn out in childbirth, as scripture requires. At thirty-two my mother has another decade of fertility ahead of her, so no wonder Sister Cora is bothered. Unfortunately, her ill temper is directed at me and all of my siblings as well.

Settling into my seat at the back of the schoolroom, I felt a flush of excitement. Standing beside Sister Emily, helping her to organize the day's lessons, was the reason I checked my hair in the mirror before school and made sure I wore my prettiest school dress: Joseph John Hilliard. Long and lean with a relaxed, easy smile, Joseph John stood a good three inches taller than the other boys his age. Now he stood out, the only boy among so many girls, but everyone knew why he was there. He had permission from my father and Uncle Kenton to give me math lessons since I have a talent with numbers. Joseph John outgrew the classes at the Zion Academy long ago and had attended public school since he was twelve. Sister Emily had nothing more to teach him since she herself was pulled out of school at thirteen to prepare for marriage, as many of my friends have been. Everyone knew that Joseph John would go on to college and become an engineer. Now I caught his eye and smiled at the way he beamed when he saw me.

Although he attended public school, Joseph John still came to class early each day to help the younger children with their numbers and letters. And once a week he went to public school for a half day, an arrangement his father had agreed upon with the prophet, so that Joseph John could do his fair share of work in the community. On that day he was allowed to sit in the back of the schoolroom with me, where Sister Emily could see and hear our lessons.

Because of my skill with figures, my father had gotten me a job working part-time after school in the Pineridge general store and I was learning how to calculate the accounts. I also was allowed to accompany Sister Cora into town to buy cloth for sewing and other staple items. There was even talk that Daddy might allow me to attend public high school and a year of community college to learn proper accounting skills that I could put to use for the community. That would be exciting, but I would be uneasy on the outside where the prophet says Satan the destroyer is always waiting to claim us.

With my mathematics book open and Joseph John settling in beside me I felt giddy at his proximity. Sitting so close, I could smell the fresh, sweet alfalfa on his clothes. His hair was a rich brown with streaks of gold from working in the sun of the rock quarry. His denim shirt had the soft, worn feel of work and many washings as it brushed up against my wrist. With our heads leaned together over the book I whispered, "Were you feeding the horses before school?"

Joseph John tried to suppress a grin. "Why? Do I smell like one?"

I kicked his foot under the table. "Not the horses, the alfalfa. It's nice," I said, careful to keep my eyes glued to my textbook but still, I saw Joseph John blush slightly.

Sister Emily passed by and fixed us with her stern, cross-eyed gaze. After she left, Joseph John said, "You know, I had that dream again. About us being married. I know it's a revelation. So, it's going to be this month."

I felt my heart beat faster but kept my voice steady. "What is?" I asked.

Joseph John dropped his voice so it was barely audible. "That I talk to my father, about you and me. Getting married. I'm eighteen now, and soon it will be your time."

I stared hard at the math figures, willing myself to stay calm, but I felt as if my heart would fly to the sun and come raining down in a million shining, happy pieces. We had whispered about it since we were children and now it was about to happen. I was going to marry Joseph John Hilliard, to be his legal wife and the envy of all the girls in Pineridge! It's a dream that I had carried inside for so long. Not just to marry the boy I love and who loves me but to be a first wife, a legal wife.

Plural marriage is one of the foundations of life in the Brotherhood of the Lord; it was canonized forever in Section 132 of the Doctrines and Covenants, one of the most important books of Mormon scripture. Multiple wives are required for a godly man to get into heaven, and the prophet regularly performs spiritual marriages, deciding who should be wed to whom, placing girls to be exalted in plural marriage based on a revelation from God. Most families wait to marry their daughters until the girl begins menstruation, as childbearing is expected within the first year of matrimony. Raising up a righteous seed unto the Lord is a woman's highest calling and it is only through a husband's guidance that a woman can attain entry into the celestial kingdom.

Being the first wife, like Sister Cora, comes with certain privileges, as the first wife is the only wife recognized by law. On state records the other sister wives use phony surnames, often chosen at random from the phone book, in order to qualify for government assistance. The agencies that dole out food stamps and other aid that the community depends on would be loathe to provide it for polygamists; the children of Pineridge know very well that they have to keep their origins hidden from prying eyes and curious Gentiles. My mother chose the last name of Robicheaux on the welfare applications for us, although of course within the community we are known as Merrills, Eldon Ray's offspring.

But my children would do no such thing, for I would be Joseph John's first and legal wife. My children would bear their father's name, they would have birth certificates, and I would have a proper marriage license. How I prayed that my monthly cycle would begin soon! As Joseph John explained how to calculate the algebra problems in the textbook, I allowed my mind to wander. How wonderful to live with Joseph John as husband and wife, to touch his hair, to feel his hands around my waist. . . .

I quickly shook such wicked thoughts away. What had come over me? I looked up to see Sister Emily watching, always watching. In league with Sister Cora, Sister Emily was always looking for a way to undermine my mother's position, and everyone knows that a woman's children are a reflection of her obedience to God's will. Sister Cora's oldest son, the first Eldon Ray Jr., as well as his brother Lamont, had run off and left the community—a source of great shame upon her.

Now my brother was called Eldon Ray Jr. and as my mother's oldest daughter, I knew that the other sister wives were hoping to catch me in some trespass. Normally I was careful to be very good at all times. I felt the heat of embarrassment rise to my face as I imagined Sister Emily reading my thoughts about Joseph John. I focused my attention on the schoolbook in front of me and kept my head down. I would kneel and pray to the Lord for a pure spirit before supper, to show God that I was worthy of His blessings.

After class it was time to go back home to help our mothers with the sewing, laundering, and cleaning. We don't have television, newspapers, or computers, but there is always a lot to do in Pineridge, what with so many children to cook and care for. Except for Rowena, who is still a baby, my younger sisters and I could probably change a dirty diaper, prepare a bottle, and soothe a colicky baby, all with one hand pumping away on the butter churn. We do the women's work; the boys help in the rock quarry or to build the new livestock barn or other physical labors.

I fell into step beside my sisters. Laura Jean, Liza, Carlene, Olive, and I walked in a group with Sister Cora's daughters while the children of the lesser wives hung back. The girls from other families flocked together, keeping a certain distance. I did my best to ignore their tittering as Joseph John ran by with a group of boys, joking and jostling one another. All the girls fancied Joseph John and were jealous of my special friendship with him, even my fourteen-year-old half sister, Leigh Ann, but she was good-natured about it, unlike Wendy Callers or Sharon Paine.

I smiled to myself, remembering the day last year when Wendy Callers had stopped me outside the temple, her pinched face even more drawn and narrow than usual, her voice filled with bitterness.

"Just know, Alva Jane, that when Joseph John is ready to

13

take a wife, he'll choose someone quiet and obedient, not a will-ful, book-smart girl like you, who holds herself up as his equal!"

"We'll see about that," I'd told her, and even then I wasn't worried. After all, my father sits on the Priesthood Council. I am a Merrill, not a Paine or a Callers or daughter of any other lesser family. And now Wendy would have to eat her words, when she learned of my pending marriage.

As we passed the large limestone residence where the prophet, Uncle Kenton, lives with his thirteen wives, Wendy Callers looked longingly after Joseph John and said in a loud voice, "I think Joseph John might be the one mighty and strong that the scriptures foretell!"

Some girls giggled loudly while others elbowed Wendy for her insolence. It was not for a girl to be speculating on scrip-ture and what God foretold, certainly not in proximity of the prophet, who spoke to God daily. He was so busy with so many important matters, but Uncle Kenton always found the time to watch us returning from our lessons at school. He stood at his open window now, resting his hands on his belly, and nodded as we walked by.

I wondered if he had heard Wendy's remark. Better not to look directly at him, not to call attention to myself. With my heart set on Joseph John, I knew it would be wise to avoid being noticed by one of the council members or other middle-aged men in the community. If one of them should have a revelation to marry a particular girl and the prophet agrees, she is sealed and her fate decided. Too many of my friends had been married off to men older than their fathers and I was determined that would not happen to me. Not that I had much to worry about. I was Daddy's favorite daughter and I knew that my father liked Joseph John, thought him to be a fine boy. I was sure he would approve of our marriage.

I smiled to myself, thinking of Joseph John seated beside me in the schoolroom and our whispered conversation. Tomorrow would be Saturday and we would have the chance to work side by side in the community garden, which was one of the only places we girls were allowed to mix with the boys, even with an elder keeping a watch over us. Soon there would be no hiding or sneaking off to meet. Soon we would be married for all to see.

The day was clear and bright, and the flowers were starting to bloom in fragile colors, incongruous against the harsh, unforgiving sun. I took a deep breath and felt the warm, dry air fill my lungs. All was well in the world.

CHAPTER TWO

THAT EVENING AFTER SUPPER MY SISTERS AND I worked on mending the boys' yard clothes while the family sat listening to Sister Emily read aloud from The Pearl of Great Price, the book of revelations of Joseph Smith. Sister Emily's voice was high and thin as she intoned the words.

"'And now it came to pass that when Moses had said those words, behold Satan came tempting him, saying Moses, son of man, worship me. And it came to pass that Moses looked upon Satan and said who art thou?'"

My oldest brother, Cliff, shifted in his seat on the sofa and I watched him with concern. Lately he had been going off with some of the Paine boys at night and they were known to be a bad influence, missing church and going into Moab to drink and associate with Gentile girls, born outside The Principle. Just today, I'd heard Daddy order Cliff to stay home this evening, and from his tone there was to be no discussion about it. I tried to catch Cliff's eye but he just stared at his feet. He needed to listen closely to what Sister Emily was reading, what the scripture lesson was teaching us. He needed to get back onto the right path but since his mind was a million miles away, the best I could do was to pray for him.

There was a knock at the door and Lucas ran to answer it. Outside, Ruby Jaynes, one of Sister Cora's many grandchildren, stood shivering on the porch. "Grandma, you got to come quick. Mama's having trouble with the baby!"

Sister Cora stood and looked to Daddy, who sat reading from an Ogden Kraut book. "May I go to our daughter's?" she asked.

Daddy nodded his approval, barely looking up. I knew my mother would go to Rita Mae's also, since she was skilled in birthing babies. But as the women stood to leave, Daddy stopped Mama with a hand on her arm.

"You're not to go," he said.

Sister Cora's eyes flashed in anger as Mama deferred to her husband with a faint smile and moved to the stairway.

"I have to bring someone with me. Rita Mae's sister wives are as thick as hammers; they won't know what to do if there's trouble," Sister Cora said.

"Then take Emily," Daddy replied. But Sister Cora would not give in that easily.

"Sister Maureen is the most knowledgeable and experienced in delivering babies, and you know our Rita Mae is not strong in childbirth," she pressed.

I knew that it must be Mama's fertile time and Daddy was going to have relations with her, free from Sister Cora's oppressive jealousy. The rivalry among the sister wives is part of all of our daily lives. I can't even count how many times I've spotted Sister Cora standing in the foyer listening for sounds of Daddy and Mama in the bedroom upstairs.

Even Mama, the clear favorite, becomes mean-tempered and impatient if Daddy spends too much time with the other sister wives. When my father returns from his weekly visit to Sister Eulalia's trailer, Mama always listens for his step on the stairs and whispers to me, "Your father is just fulfilling his duty to the doctrine of plural marriage. You can see there is no love or desire there."

Sister Eulalia is still young but she's rather slow-witted. Mama has nothing to fear from her.

Daddy's fifth wife, Sister Susannah, became heavyset after the birth of her twins, her skin feels clammy to the touch, and her face is always covered with a sheen of sweat. I know she does not hold much attraction for Daddy. He goes to her trailer once or twice a month at most.

Sister Sherrie, the third wife, is just two years older than Mama but she looks like a dried-up stick of grass, with her bony frame and paper-thin skin. Her eyebrows long ago disappeared and have never grown back. She lives at the very back of the property in the lumber shed that has been converted. She has only one son, Orton, who is now twenty-one and away on his mission. She hemorrhaged so badly in childbirth that she could not have any others. Knowing that she was not doing her duty to the Lord and her husband made her melancholy; she keeps to herself and the other wives let her be. My father rarely visits her, as sexual relations with a woman who is infertile, menstruating, or past her time are strictly prohibited.

When Sister Mona joined the family, I think Mama was worried since Sister Mona was just sixteen then and quite pretty, with striking black hair and a womanly figure. But Sister Mona suffers with her nerves and is often too depressed even to take care of two-year-old Cindy, so it falls to Sister Emily. Sister Mona is prone to crying and getting so emotional that Daddy's visits to her are not always happy. I have seen him return from her trailer to the main house in a high temper more than once, cursing under his breath. On those evenings Mama takes it upon herself to soothe his spirit and satisfy his manly desires, as is a woman's duty.

Daddy visits Mama's bed regularly and that translates to power for my mother. He clearly spends more time with Mama than Sister Cora thinks appropriate, especially for a fourth wife.

Each wife has her designated night with Daddy so that he can fulfill his duties and spread his seed, building up his heavenly kingdom according to scripture. But on off-nights, when Daddy comes back late from council meetings, he often slips quietly into our room and finds Mama behind the curtain she hung to provide him with some privacy. If I am awake, I try to keep my eyes closed and turn to the wall to block out the sounds of their coupling. There is no talk between them, just the sounds of clothing being removed and the squeaking of the bedsprings. Once, when I was younger, the curtain moved and I caught a glimpse of naked flesh, of bodies entwined, and it made me feel unsettled. When that happened I pulled the covers over my head and shut my eyes tight, feeling guilty for having seen something I shouldn't have.

My father visits Mama so often that I have grown accustomed to the rhythm of their encounters: the slapping sound of my mother's flesh and their exertion. Sometimes Daddy's breath comes so ragged and guttural he sounds like a green horse being broke to saddle. I can't help but wonder if my own intimate moments with Joseph John will be like that, wordless and urgent? I have learned from my mother that men have strong needs to be met and it is a woman's duty to fulfill them. After all, the husband is the family priesthood head and it is only through his guidance that wives are exalted and shown the path to heaven.

After finishing with Mama, my father always returns to Sister Cora's room to sleep until morning, a respect for her status as his first wife. But Sister Cora still seethes over Daddy's obvious preference for my mother's bed.

I looked up from my sewing to see my mother, Daddy, and Sister Cora, like points on a triangle at the foot of the stairs. It was clear that Daddy would not give in to Sister Cora and allow Mama to go to Rita Mae's. Even though Mama kept her eyes down, I could see that she was smiling, happy to have another triumph over Sister Cora. Watching Mama disappear silently up the stairs and Sister Cora's face as she saw the futility of struggling against her husband's desire, I felt a stab of pity for her. It must be hard to be past an age and time when she could kindle her husband's affections. Soon Daddy wouldn't have relations with her at all.

"So, am I to go alone to Rita Mae's, then?" Sister Cora tried one last time.

"Take Alva; it's time she learned how to birth babies," Daddy said over his shoulder.

He was brusque, more so than usual. Lately things had been tense around the house and in the community at large. There had been more council meetings, more precautions taken to safeguard the community. That meant there must be some fear of a raid, of legal action against the Brotherhood by outsiders. It is a constant undercurrent to our lives but at times more palpable than others. Daddy's tone with Sister Cora was probably a symptom of other distractions troubling him. But my pity for Sister Cora didn't last long when she grabbed my arm roughly and ordered, "Get your sweater, Alva Jane. I'll need help and an extra set of hands."

I didn't want to go, I didn't like going to Rita Mae's house but knew better than to protest when Sister Cora was angry. Like Sister Cora and Sister Emily, Rita Mae and her sister Rayanne had married the same man, Donald Dean Jaynes, a third cousin of my mother's. He was known to be difficult and unpredictable and I always felt uneasy when he came into the general store.

Donald Dean's first wife had taken her own life and the second one, Juleen, had run off. I had heard the sister wives speaking in hushed tones of Juleen, who had fallen so far from grace after leaving Pineridge that she sold her body to Gentiles to survive. Sister Emily said that Juleen had even been seen in the city with a black man. The punishment for having sexual relations with the Seed of Cain was swift and merciless: God would strike you dead on the spot. I figured that Juleen had suffered just such a fate.

Rita Mae got on fine but since her marriage Rayanne had become, as Mama described her, "touched in the head." The last time I had been to visit, Rayanne sat silently in a chair in the kitchen, sorting plastic food containers and lids, placing them neatly in drawers. She had managed to have fourteen children, a sign that she was able to do her duty to her husband, but the other sister wives had to care for them.

Unlike Rayanne, Rita Mae always had a difficult time in childbirth. Married at fifteen, now thirty years old, she had only five living children. Her last two babies had come stillborn.

When I was four years old, Mama took me to help with the birth of Rita Mae's youngest daughter, Marianne. I may have been young but I remember well the fear and tension that filled the room when the baby's little feet came out first. Sister Cora had pushed and prodded Rita Mae's belly, trying to shift the baby inside. I was dumbstruck at the amount of blood that saturated the sheets; it had seemed enough to fill a river. When it was over, my hands became chapped and raw from rinsing them repeatedly in cold water.

Since then I've heard of other babies that came backward and Mama says it is because there is something crooked in the mother's spirit, that her faith is not strong and God is giving her a trial to set her on the right path. The only doctor that a pregnant woman is allowed to see in Pineridge is Doc Levi, who didn't go to a school to learn about medicine. His father had the gift and passed it on to his son. Besides, Mama has told me many times that the Gentile doctors cannot be trusted. They only want women to have three or four children and they will give you a hysterectomy or some other abomination to render you infertile during an exam. So, what woman who wants to fulfill her duty to her husband and the Lord would take such a risk?

Little Marianne is as perfect and beautiful as a doll with her blond curls and enormous blue eyes, but she is behind in her mental development. Now at ten years old she is docile and quiet, speaking just a few basic words, easily confused and frightened by things she does not understand. I've always had a soft spot for her, perhaps from having witnessed her difficult arrival into this world.

I hurried, following Sister Cora into the cool night air to make the trek to Rita Mae's house. The sky was covered in stars, so thick and brilliant it looked as if God had spilled a pile of diamonds across the heavens. I looked up and wondered what it would be like to be swallowed up among them, floating in their endless, infinite brightness.

"Pay attention to where you're walking. The last thing we need is for you to twist an ankle and not be a help to anyone!" Sister Cora chastised.

I lowered my eyes and walked a few paces behind Sister Cora the rest of the way. We found Rita Mae prone in bed, moaning as the contractions came. Several of Rita Mae's sister wives and a few young girls, including Marianne, hovered helplessly. Donald Dean sat beside the bed with his sleeves rolled up.

"How long has she been at it?" Sister Cora asked.

"Since early this morning, around five," Donald Dean replied.

"Has her water broken?"

"About three hours ago."

Sister Cora's face darkened; three hours was too long to wait. But she held her tongue. No matter how upset she was, I knew that she would not dare to speak up to any priesthood head in the community. Rita Mae looked about ready to pass out. I felt the clutch of anxiety in my throat as Rita Mae reached for her mother's hand, her breathing hard and shallow. A cousin of Mama's had died in childbirth and the idea of that scared the spirit right out of me.

"That's it, breathe in and out, in and out. . . ." Sister Cora spoke quietly. "You have hot water and disinfectant, Brother Donald?"

"Water's boiling on the stove. I have the alcohol right here," he replied, the sweat visible on his forehead.

"Alva, get some fresh cotton cloths from the linen closet. And the washtub," Sister Cora ordered. She began massaging Rita Mae, and I was happy to leave the heavy scent of sweat and fear that filled the room. Marianne trailed behind me.

"Come on, pretty baby, help cousin Alva with the cotton for Mommy," I said. *Why did they bring Marianne to the birth?* I thought. She couldn't understand what was going on except that her mother was in trouble and everyone was nervous. She didn't need to be there witnessing her mother's suffering.

As I climbed on the step stool to retrieve the clean linens, I heard a stirring of activity from the bedroom. "Hurry, Alva! I think the baby's coming!" Sister Cora called out.

I ran back with the cloths, almost colliding with one of Rayanne's daughters carrying a large pot of boiling water from the kitchen. Rita Mae cried out in pain, arching her hips and drawing her knees up. In a gush of milky, blood-streaked fluid, the baby's head began to emerge.

"Push, hard now," Sister Cora directed, but as much as Rita Mae pushed, the baby did not move any farther. Just the very crown of the head was visible and Rita Mae was hovering at the edge of consciousness, covered in sweat. Sister Cora rolled up her sleeves and reached for the baby, sliding her hands around the scalp and giving a light tug. I knew this was not good, that the baby should move out easily now. I prayed that this would not be a stillborn baby, that we would not have to bury another tiny body in a small white coffin.

"It's not coming," Sister Cora said.

"I'm not losing another one," Donald Dean said as Rita Mae shuddered and gave a quick thrust, pushing the baby out a few inches more.

Marianne began to cry and Sister Cora barked at me, "Take Marianne out of here!"

I was only too happy to oblige, leading Marianne away down the hall and toward the front porch. As I pushed open the screen door, we heard Rita Mae scream once and then fall into silence. I saw the fear in Marianne's eyes and pulled her onto my lap to comfort her.

*   *   *

On the walk back home, Sister Cora was quiet, her sweater wrapped tightly, her arms crossed. Rita Mae had not regained consciousness, even after the other girls and I had stripped the bed and rinsed the bloody sheets in the washtub, but the baby had been born alive. As we left, Donald Dean had thanked Sister Cora and assured her, "We'll pray for her recovery. But be pleased that she's done her duty to the Lord, Sister. One child is worth ten of the mother."

I didn't try to talk with Sister Cora. We walked side by side, locked in silence and our own thoughts. I tried to push from my mind the image of Rita Mae, unmoving and limp.

Just remembering the metallic smell of the blood and the stickiness of it on my hands made my stomach queasy and nauseous. What would happen if I were weak in childbirth like Rita Mae? What if I were unable to give Joseph John a baby a year as the prophet expected? What if I fell from favor like my father's lesser wives, and ended up pushed aside and living on the leftovers of Joseph John's love and attention? It was a fate too terrible to imagine.

I resolved to seek my mother's counsel once my marriage was arranged. I would pray to the Lord to make me fertile and abundant. I would learn the secrets that had made my mother the favorite, how to please a man and hold his affections, and I would put them to use.

The next morning I was to work in the community garden with the other teenagers under the watch of my father's cousin, Uncle Luther. The boys and girls work in separate rows, but Uncle Luther is often too distracted to be strict with the rules. Every Saturday we till the soil and mix in mulch, coaxing vegetables to grow in the sandy ground under a shade canopy. Each family in Pineridge plants their own vegetable garden as well, but none is abundant given the withering heat. The community garden is to help those who have little or no harvest from their home vegetable patch.

After baking the bread and tending to my younger siblings, I bathed and changed into a good work dress, a pretty shade of green that I hoped would set off my eyes. I braided my damp hair and snuck a dab of my mother's petroleum jelly to put on my lips and eyelashes. I knew vanity was a sin of pride but I also knew Joseph John would be there and I convinced myself that God would not begrudge me a little extra shine.

Like he did every Saturday, Joseph John would be safe-guarding the spot beside him especially for me. We would be able to whisper about our plans safe from Sister Emily's eagle eye. Supervising the youngsters was Uncle Luther's only responsibility, since his mind wandered and he was prone to walk off.

When I arrived at the garden, sure enough, I saw Joseph John seated with a spade, working on a row of root vegetables, an empty spot in the row beside him. My heart quickened, wondering if he had spoken to his father about our marriage yet.

"I have something to show you, Alva. Something big!" Joseph John said as I settled in to work.

"What is it?"

He reached into the pocket of his pants and pulled out a folded envelope, handing it to me. "Go ahead, open it up," he said with a smile.

I unfolded the paper inside and saw the letterhead of Brigham Young University. My eyes scanned the page:

Dear Mr. Hilliard,

We are writing to inform you of your acceptance into Brigham Young University for the coming school year.

I beamed at Joseph John. He was going to college! I handed the paper back to him and he quickly pocketed it. Two rows over, Wendy Callers was looking at us intently, her eyes narrowed into little slits. Joseph John dropped his voice to whisper, "I want to have the prophet marry us before I start school in the fall. I'm going ask permission to have you come with me to Provo as my wife."

My heart thrilled at the idea of it! To go and live as a proper married couple, to take care of Joseph John while he pursued his studies, would be a dream come true. I doubted, however, that my father would agree to it. More likely, we would wed and I would remain within the community for a few more years. Either way, I would be one step closer to adulthood and doing my duty to the Lord and my husband.

Wendy Callers moved next to me, clearly trying to eavesdrop, and Joseph John took that as his cue to move away to another row of the garden. Wendy's eyes followed him.

"What was that Joseph John showed you?" she asked.

"It was just the figures for the algebra he's been teaching me. There were some problems I couldn't figure out," I fibbed, tossing a skinny radish into a basket.

"It didn't look like figures to me."

I just smiled at her as I rose and took my basket to follow Joseph John. I would not let Wendy Callers and her snooping ruin my happiness at our good news.

CHAPTER THREE

WHEN I RETURNED HOME THE NEXT DAY AFTER
school I was surprised to find a stranger sitting in the living
room with my mother, Sister Cora, and Sister Emily, sipping a
cup of apple tea. She was a woman, around Sister Susannah's
age, dressed in Gentile clothes. Her blond hair was short and
smooth, as shiny as satin. She wore a wedding band and a spar-
kling diamond ring and a braided gold bracelet. I hung back in
the doorway, watching her with her sparkly jewelry so unlike
anything worn by the women in Pineridge. Mama spotted me
and called me into the sitting room.

"This is my oldest daughter, Alva Jane," she said proudly. I
shook the woman's hand gently and took a seat at my mother's feet.

"This is Brenda Norton. She and her husband, Jack, are joining the community," Sister Cora explained.

Sister Cora's tone was polite but I could see the caution in her eyes. Outsiders were rare within our compound walls.

Mrs. Norton broke into a big smile but there was a lackluster quality to her eyes, as if the top half of her face did not agree with the bottom. I nodded politely but I still felt uncertain about her. Almost everyone in Pineridge had been born into the Brotherhood of the Lord, the true religion, and the principle of plural marriage. I had met outsiders before, of course, when I accompanied Sister Cora into town for supplies. But I had never spoken to one beyond making a simple purchase. It's strictly forbidden. Mrs. Norton was the first outsider I had ever met inside the walls of Pineridge.

"Jack and I want a more traditional way of life," Mrs. Norton said. "We both feel a lack of religious integrity in the mainline Mormon Church. Too many covenants have been broken. It's important to be a living example of the scriptures."

"Amen to that," Mama affirmed, as she reached out to smooth some wayward pieces of hair into my braid.

Mrs. Norton continued, "Living The Principle is something we both felt we needed to fulfill God's plan for us."

Sister Cora smiled. I have heard the sister wives discuss how couples that have never followed the true religion and have lived in monogamy often don't understand the necessity of plural marriage to their salvation. They have problems adjusting to it. Sister Cora reached out and took my mother's hand in hers, which surprised me since their dislike of one another was so strong. But I understood she was putting on a good face for an outsider, something we had all been taught to do.

31

"The Principle at work is a blessing and a joy. In our family there are seven sister wives and the love among us is a salve to the daily trials of a woman's life." Sister Cora nodded knowingly at Mrs. Norton, who responded in kind.

Sister Emily interjected, "What kind of work does your husband do?"

"He's a contractor. Uncle Kenton seems to have a lot of plans that Jack can help out with. I work at the Bank of Utah. I was at the branch in Provo but I just switched to the Moab branch when we decided to come to Pineridge."

I turned to look at her. "No women here have jobs," I said.

Most don't have time for anything more than keeping their houses, sewing the family's clothes, cooking, canning, baking, raising the children, and other duties. Plus the outside world is filled with temptations and subversive ideas meant to lead a woman away from her godly path. I've heard the prophet say it a hundred times.

Sister Cora shot me a hard look as Mrs. Norton said, "Well, I've been working at the bank since I got out of BYU and I have quite a good position. So I plan to stay on as long as they'll have me."

I gasped, unable to hide my surprise. I had only met a couple of women who had finished public high school and never met any who had gone to college, especially BYU where Joseph John would be going in the fall.

"You went to Brigham Young University? What's it like? Is it very big?" I asked her.

My mother put a hand on my shoulder, a signal for me to

stop talking. "Forgive my daughter for her inappropriate questions, Mrs. Norton. She doesn't meet many people outside the community and she doesn't know what is proper conversation among women."

I felt the color rise to my cheeks.

Mrs. Norton smiled. "Oh, I don't find her questions inappropriate at all, Mrs. Merrill. I think it's normal that a young girl would be interested in college life and things like that."

I don't know where Mrs. Norton got her ideas from, but in Pineridge girls don't think about college. That was only for the boys and very few of them went that far in their education. Even though my daddy sometimes talked of me going to the community college for a year, I didn't believe it would happen. I couldn't imagine going to a university myself, sitting in rooms full of strangers and Gentiles, boys and girls all mixed up together.

"Maybe girls on the outside are interested in those things, Mrs. Norton, but here in Pineridge there's no use in filling their heads with ideas that lead them away from their duty to God," Sister Emily said.

Mrs. Norton looked flustered for a moment and then Mama asked, "How many children do you and your husband have?"

Mrs. Norton set down her teacup. "We don't have any yet."

I looked at her closely, figuring her to be in her late twenties. Having no children at that age was unheard of, unless there was something wrong, like with Sister Sherrie after Orton's birth. That must be why she had a job; she had nothing else to do. I felt pity and then a stab of anxiety. What if I turned out to be like Brenda Norton, childless with a tight smile and a hollow look to her eyes?

Sister Cora smiled reassuringly at Mrs. Norton, "God has his own timetable for all of us on our path to salvation. Your time will come, dear."

Mrs. Norton looked as if she would burst into tears. She checked her watch and I saw that her hand was trembling. "I really should get back. Jack must be done touring the temple with your husband," she said. She looked around as if she didn't know which sister wife to direct her words to, which made me smile inside.

My mother rose and put an arm around Mrs. Norton's shoulder as the sister wives accompanied her to the door. "I'll send Alva around to help you get accustomed to Pineridge and all our funny ways," she said, crinkling her nose playfully. "She's a good girl and an example of the Lord's work in the Brotherhood, free of the vices that afflict so many young people today."

When Mama and Sister Cora started down the path toward the front gate with Mrs. Norton, Sister Emily caught my arm. "What do you think you're doing, asking about her job and college?" she said.

"I was just making conversation." Sister Emily was always in a foul temper and today was no different.

"You don't know anything about that Brenda Norton. She could be a fake, sent to get information on the Brotherhood. And you, just talking a blue streak like you were grown!"

I pulled my arm away from Sister Emily's bony grip.

I didn't care if I got in trouble for being willful. I ran out to join my mother and Sister Cora. As I got there, Wendy Callers approached, with a fresh pound cake wrapped in a checkered towel.

"This is for you, Sister Cora," she said sweetly.

"How lovely is that? A pound cake and it's still warm!" Sister Cora said, "Mrs. Norton, I'd like you to meet Wendy Callers, another fine young girl in our community. This is Brenda Norton; she and her husband will be moving into the old DeLory house."

Mitch DeLory had argued with the prophet last year and been expelled from the community. His wives and children had been reassigned to another man, but the house he built still stood empty because DeLory had gotten a lawyer and tried to go to court just to stir up trouble.

"I can't get over how well brought up the girls are here," Mrs. Norton remarked.

"We keep sweet, no matter what!" Wendy said with a smile.

I took my mother's hand while we all stood together and waved as Mrs. Norton passed through the front gate. Then Wendy asked, "May I speak to you in the kitchen, Sister Cora?"

I paid no attention when they headed inside. I was watching Mrs. Norton disappear down the block with her sleek hair and her pretty blue suit. I felt a little nervous about visiting with her, if Mama was telling the truth about me helping her learn the ways of the community. But it would give me the chance to ask her about Brigham Young University and life in Provo without Mama and the other sister wives listening in.

I entered the house and headed toward the back porch where we were to haul the rugs for summer cleaning, but I stopped outside the kitchen when I heard Wendy Callers's voice.

"And it's not the first time I've seen Alva Jane talking in secret like that with Joseph John. We all know he's sweet on her and she seems to feel the same."

Sister Cora clucked her tongue disapprovingly and then Sister Emily dropped her voice to say something I couldn't hear, but I got the gist of it. Wendy Callers was tattling, trying to make trouble for Joseph John and me! Even though my temper flared, I was happy to hear her say what my heart knew to be true, that we were sweet on each other. I considered running into the kitchen to defend myself but I knew Sister Cora wouldn't take kindly to eavesdropping.

Besides, Wendy was wasting her time tattling to Sister Cora. My father was the rod and the rule in our house and once he agreed to my marriage with Joseph John, there was nothing any of them could do to stop it. Even if Sister Cora was always looking for a way to make me and Mama look bad, I had done nothing wrong. I walked past the kitchen door and nodded to Wendy, paying her idle gossip no mind.

It was still dark outside when I arose the next morning and padded silently to the bathroom to get ready for a busy day. Along with my regular chores at home, on Friday afternoons I work in the Pineridge store, helping Mr. Battle, whose eyes are starting to go bad.

The night before, my father had come home from the

council meeting and announced that the prophet had decreed that today there would be baptisms of the dead. Baptizing in death those unfortunate souls who did not find the true religion while they were alive is one of the most important rituals in Pineridge. It is the saints' responsibility to complete God's work and make sure that every soul is baptized into the Mormon faith.

Many times I have helped my mother and the other sister wives pore over registration lists from Catholic and Protestant parishes and Jewish synagogues to find the names of those who have died unsaved. Today in the temple, the saints would line up and climb the gilded steps on either side of the large baptismal font, which sits atop statues of twelve oxen, gathered into a circle to represent the twelve tribes of Israel. Each saint would stand before the prophet and other council members to offer him- or herself as a proxy to be baptized for the lost soul, immersed in the holy waters.

I knew it was a responsibility and an honor to save those locked in a death prison by their misguided faith, but I wished it didn't have to be today. Baptism of the dead sometimes took hours, depending on the fervor of the prophet and the revelation he had received. With that and my work at the store, there would hardly be time to stop by Mrs. Norton's like Mama had asked me to, to see if they were really moving in today.

Downstairs I could hear Mama preparing the loaf pans for the daily bread making. Perhaps I would make an extra loaf today to take over to Mrs. Norton, along with some of my mother's butter. Mrs. Norton probably didn't know how to churn butter and would need someone to show her how. If she didn't sew, she'd also need someone to help her make some proper dresses. She certainly couldn't continue wearing those modern clothes in Pineridge. There was a lot to teach her and it looked as if it would fall to me. I didn't mind. Industriousness is a virtue and I knew God would reward me for it.

As I splashed my face with cold water, my sister Leigh Ann, Sister Cora's daughter, came in and quickly stripped off her long cotton nightgown and her sacred undergarments. Standing naked in the chilly bathroom, Leigh Ann's pale skin erupted in goose bumps and her teeth chattered. She rinsed the white night dress and the sacred undergarments out in the sink. I saw a dark red stain begin to bleed in the cold water and disappear down the drain.

"Did your cycle come again?" I whispered. Leigh Ann had started her cycle a few months earlier, just before turning fifteen. This morning she looked pale and sick with dark circles under her eyes.

She nodded. "It came in the middle of the night and I couldn't find the cotton pads so I bled all over my nightgown and my undergarments. If my mom sees it she'll whip me for sure!"

Leigh Ann scrubbed the stains with bar soap. I helped her until we had washed the stain out completely. Leigh Ann let out a sigh of relief and giggled when she saw her reflection in the mirror. "Look at me, standing here buck naked, freezing cold, washing like a crazy woman!"

"How does it feel this time?" I asked.

Leigh Ann suffered terrible cramps each time her cycle came; last month she had even thrown up while we were peeling potatoes and Sister Cora had gotten after her with the switch for that, raising angry red welts on her legs.

"It hurts something awful. I don't know how I'm going to get through the baptism of the dead today." She sighed.

Leigh Ann went to make up her bed and tidy her room and I put on my own fresh undergarments. I carefully inspected the undergarment I had removed to be washed and saw with dismay that it was close to worn out, the seams fraying and the white cotton faded to a pale gray. I would ask her mother for help in removing the sacred symbols from the breasts, navel, and knees so that it could be burned, as is required for the destruction of all holy relics. In my new, crisp undergarment, I felt safe, knowing I was protected from bullets, fire, knives, and all manner of evil—and more importantly, from Satan, the destroyer. I laid out my white temple garments to put on after bread making since there would be no school today.

After completing my chores, I went to the temple with my sisters. I prayed fervently for the newly baptized, watching as the saints lined up for the soul saving. Everyone emerged wet from head to toe after immersion on the baptismal font. I was the proxy for two Catholic women named Mary Williams and Collette McCann, now baptized in death as Latter Day Saints. Afterward, I raced home to retrieve the fresh bread to take to Mrs. Norton before going to help Mr. Battle at the store.

At home I found Sister Cora alone in the kitchen. I

wrapped up the bread in an embroidered cloth and was ready to leave when she said, "I saw the Hilliards at the baptisms this morning. That Joseph John seems like a fine young man."

"Yes, he is. He's quite a good student, too," I said.

"I hear he goes to the public school over in Moab. His father says the boy wants to be an engineer."

"That's right, Sister Cora."

"It seems you know quite a bit about it." Sister Cora glanced sideways at me and I regretted having said anything at all. "Well, he's a handsome boy," she continued. "I'm sure that when he's out in the big world away from our little paradise here in Pineridge he'll find some Gentile girl. It always happens that way with the ones who leave the community."

I did my best to hide it but Sister Cora's words cut me to the quick. She might as well have slapped me. Of course Joseph John would be meeting college girls next year, girls who wore modern clothes and drove cars. Girls who listened to poplar radio music and read newspapers. I knew there was a different world outside the limestone walls that held us safe in the community. He was exposed to those things in public high school each day, but he came home to our life in Pineridge every afternoon. Next year it would be different, he would live at the university. Joseph John would be part of the outside world and I would be part of the one he left behind. Even if we were married already, he might come to regret it.

I hated how my voice sounded rubbery and thick when I asked, "Do you really think so, Sister Cora?"

Sister Cora smiled and nodded, clearly satisfied with herself.

Then she took the loaf of bread from my hands, inspecting the cloth that covered it. "It's wasteful to give that fine embroidery to the Nortons. We don't even know how long they'll last here in the community," she admonished.

"My mother thought it would be nice to bring a little something to welcome them," I replied, still trying to shake from my head the image of Joseph John surrounded by Gentile girls in blue jeans.

Sister Cora snapped back at me, "Giving them the bread and butter of our labors is enough. Your mother is too free with everything, it seems."

I know better than to respond when Sister Cora is in one of her moods. Sometimes she sinks into a black humor so quickly that I have no idea it has happened until I see her coming at me with the switch. Still, I felt my anger rise. I was tired of Sister Cora's snide remarks about my mother; I knew it was the result of her jealousy that my father preferred Mama to her. I hoped that Daddy would visit Mama again that evening, just so I could see the frustration on Sister Cora's face.

Keep sweet, I told myself, walking out the door and leaving Sister Cora and her ill temper behind me. I carried the bread still wrapped in the towel Mama had intended. I would follow her directions; after all, *she* was my mother, not Sister Cora.

A few minutes later I was at the door of the old DeLory house. When Mrs. Norton answered, I swallowed my surprise to see her in pants and a plain shirt with a pair of flat tennis shoes on her feet. How did she expect to join our community if she didn't even dress like us?

I handed her the loaf of bread and the butter. "I helped my mother make the bread this morning. She churned the butter last night."

"Oh, I haven't made bread in years and I've never churned butter! I used to bake with my mother when I was a little girl but it's been a while. You'll have to give me the recipe," Mrs. Norton said, ushering me in. Her house was filled with boxes and other moving supplies.

"I can do that, I make fourteen loaves with my mother every day before school."

"Fourteen loaves every day? Is it for the bakery?"

"Oh, no. It's for our family. My father has seven wives and twenty-nine children. We eat a lot of bread."

"I suppose you must," Mrs. Norton remarked. "What do you do for fun at your age in Pineridge?"

I stared at her. "Fun?"

"Sure, fun. When I was your age in Salt Lake, my sister and I used to go to the local swimming pool with our friends. Sometimes we'd go to the matinee movies downtown on Saturday."

I didn't know how to reply. We work all day. God has a purpose and a plan for us that do not involve idle play. And there are no movie houses or swimming pools in Pineridge. Sometimes we're allowed to splash around in the wash after a summer storm, but we still wear our long dresses in the water. And none of us would be allowed to socialize with boys without adult supervision. I thought again of Joseph John with those Gentile girls at college.

"Mrs. Norton, did you go swimming or to the movies with boys?"

"Sure we did. It wasn't as if anything happened. After all, we were all good Mormon kids. We didn't even have Coca-Cola to drink. And please call me Brenda. *Mrs.* Norton makes me sound like Jack's mother!"

She smiled at me and I did my best to smile back to be polite. I was taught to call grown-ups by Mister and Missus or Brother and Sister, but if she wanted me to call her Brenda, I would try.

"I've never had a Coca-Cola either," I said.

Brenda led me into the kitchen where there were boxes of dishes and all kinds of appliances that we don't use at home. "I know we're not supposed to drink caffeine or alcohol or any of that and I agree that those things can poison the body. But I will admit that I have snuck a Coke once in a while. Not with my husband around, of course."

I was stunned. "And?"

She leaned in close. "And it is so good I can see why it is a sin! Cold and sweet, with a little kick to it. Sometimes the bubbles go down just the right way and it's like nothing else!"

I tried to cover my surprise. I couldn't imagine ever breaking the rules that way. "I have a couple of cans stashed away here, if you ever get the urge to try!"

I couldn't believe what she was saying, putting temptation so squarely in my path. In my house we never broke any of the covenants. I was certain that my parents and the other sister wives had never had a drop of alcohol or caffeine or anything else prohibited. What was Mrs. Norton thinking, bringing Coca-Cola into Pineridge and offering it to me? What if I tattled on her like Wendy Callers? Or if the prophet found out? She had to be a lot more careful if she was going to join the Brotherhood of the Lord. You couldn't just say or do whatever you wanted. Maybe she truly was a spy like Sister Emily suspected.

"Is it true that there is temptation everywhere on the outside?" I asked. "The prophet says that people are living in great sin, that the Gentiles are destined to perdition. He said that even the Seed of Cain are allowed into the mainstream Mormon temples!"

Mrs. Norton looked at me, pressing her lips together, like she had words there, trying to get out. Then she said, "On the outside, people no longer refer to blacks as the Seed of Cain, Alva. That is an old belief from another time, when there was a great deal of prejudice and discrimination in the church."

"But they are descendants of the Lamanintes, they are evil. That is why God cursed them with black skin!" I exclaimed.

"I don't think that's true, Alva. And most of the LDS Church doesn't think that either. There are even African-American saints. I used to share an office with a wonderful black girl at the bank in Salt Lake who was LDS."

Brenda had been friendly, and even shared an office, with a Seed of Cain! I didn't know what to say or think, but I knew she needed some advice.

"You better not mention that to anyone here in Pineridge, Brenda. That could cause you some big problems. And you're going to have to get some proper dresses, too. You can't wear those modern clothes here if you want to fit in."

She sighed. "I figured as much. Perhaps you can help me? I don't sew that well either."

"If my mother gives me permission. It would have to be after I finish my home chores."

"Thank you. Now I have a question for you, Alva. How does plural marriage really work? Is it true what Cora said? That all the wives get along well and everyone is happy?"

I didn't know what to say and pretended I was busy with a loose button on my sleeve. In the Brotherhood we answered a higher call, to keep the spiritual laws of plural marriage even if they were against the laws of the state. If Sister Emily was right and Brenda was a spy, it would be dangerous to talk about The Principle with her. But if she was genuine and really wanted to fit in, wasn't it my responsibility to help her?

I looked at her carefully. She had a nervous smile that made me feel sorry for her. If she were a spy, I didn't think she would have been so reckless as to tell me about the Coca-Cola. More likely she just had no idea how things worked and she needed help, like Mama said. And I needed to ask her about life in Provo, about BYU, so I would have some idea what to expect when Joseph John went there in the fall. No one else in Pineridge could tell me. She clearly needed my help and I needed something from her, too. I knew I should tell her the truth.

"Well, sometimes there are disagreements. Some wives are jealous of others. It can be hard for a man to meet his obligations to spread his seed among many wives, as the Lord commanded."

Her eyes got a funny look in them. "I was just wondering . . . ," she started to say but stopped when the front door opened and her husband stepped inside. Jack Norton was tall and stocky with short, sandy brown hair and blue eyes.

"Hi, honey, this is Alva. She's Eldon Ray Merrill's daughter."

"Nice to meet you, Alva," he said, shaking my hand firmly. He smiled but something in it made me uncomfortable. His teeth were big and square and his lips slid over them too easily, like a crocodile. He put his arm around Brenda's shoulder and continued, "You'll see my wife here might need a little fashion help! And a few cooking lessons too!"

Brenda laughed, but again I noticed that her eyes didn't match her smile. "Alva is going to help me with some of those things. She makes fourteen loaves of bread every day before school; can you believe it?"

"Well, that's why we're here. The industriousness of the fundamentalist way of life is what we were missing," Mr. Norton said.

I didn't want to stay any longer and I was due at the store. "Mr. Battle must be waiting for me," I said, moving to the door.

"You'll come back again soon, won't you Alva? I so enjoyed visiting with you," Brenda said.

"Of course. I'll come by real soon."

"We'd sure like that," Mr. Norton said with the same crocodile smile, holding the door for me.

Out on the street, I turned to wave to the Nortons, who stood on the front porch watching me go. I hadn't had the chance to ask her about BYU, but maybe next time I would.

I wasn't so nervous now about visiting with her. It was a good thing they had joined the Brotherhood; she needed a little guidance but she seemed as nice as pie.

I did my best to shake off the odd feeling I had when I met Jack Norton. He was a good, God-fearing man. Daddy had said so the night before. I resolved to pray for a gentle and willing heart when it came to helping Brenda and to be cleansed of any doubt.

CHAPTER FOUR

AT THE PINERIDGE STORE, I MANNED THE CASH register, taking money and scrip while Mr. Battle directed the stockroom boys in filling the shelves. It made me proud, knowing that I was considered responsible enough to have a real job. Mr. Battle's eyes were getting bad and he needed more help with the accounts each week. We had deliveries from Moab, and some from as far away as Salt Lake, to keep the shelves stocked with the items our community needed.

Lately Mr. Battle had been showing me how to hide some of the profits and make it seem as if the store were always operating at a loss, thereby paying fewer taxes. I knew there was no shame in this. In Pineridge there are many ways to avoid paying taxes to the corrupt federal government that has persecuted us for so many years. It is a fine and honorable thing to bleed the beast, as we call it. But today there would be no bookkeeping. I hadn't been at the store an hour when Leigh Ann came running through the doorway, breathless.

"Alva, you have to come home right now. The prophet has called all council member families to a special meeting at his compound!"

Mr. Battle looked up and waved me away with a shaky, liver-spotted hand. "You go on, Alva Jane. If the prophet is having council members at his house, it's something big!" he said.

I took off my work smock and followed Leigh Ann. The prophet regularly called community gatherings to address issues that he felt needed to be dealt with collectively by the saints. Last year, he had assembled everyone to announce that he had received a revelation from God that the people of Pineridge were too covetous and materialistic. He'd had all of our belongings confiscated and stored in a grain silo, only to be returned piece by piece over time as we demonstrated our devotion. It had been a trial to cook and clean without utensils, to get by with one dress and sit on the floor with no furniture, but it had been necessary to prove our worthiness to the Lord. But a meeting of just the council families? And Leigh Ann and I were to be included? That was not usual. I hurried behind her.

"What is it? A revelation?" I asked.

"I don't think so. The sister wives have been talking all after-noon, whispering and shaking their heads. I think someone did something bad."

Back at home I saw that Leigh Ann was right; the sister

wives were gathered in the kitchen, murmuring among themselves. "What's happened, Mama?" I asked.

My mother didn't have a chance to answer before Sister
Emily stepped in. "Don't be asking questions that don't concern
you. Let it be enough that you're included in a council family
meeting rather than left at home to watch the children."

I didn't let her bother me; she was often so rude and abrupt.
Besides, she was right: The important thing was that Leigh Ann
and I were being included in a gathering—inside the prophet's
private home, no less. Just last year we would have stayed home
to read scripture with the younger kids. It meant that we were
old enough to be taken seriously.

Walking in a group with Leigh Ann and the sister wives,
I saw the other council families heading toward the prophet's
imposing compound. It was three stories high with quarters on
the left and right, shaped like an *L*. We took our place in the line
of people filing in and I looked up at the carvings on the temple
next door with the All-Seeing Eye of God above each tower, and
the five-pointed stars of the priesthood set into the limestone.

I love the temple, it is so beautiful. At the base of each
buttress are the earth stones, the footstools of the Lord, and
above them the moonstones, sunstones, and cloud stones. The
clasped right hands carved into the exterior walls of the temple
represent the right hands of fellowship cited in Galatians and
Jeremiah. Its splendor is a true testament to God's greatness.

Mixed in the crowd of council families, I felt as if the air was
alive with electricity. When we reached the front of the line, we
were greeted by several of the prophet's wives, who led us down

a stairway to a large, plain room filled with folding chairs facing a raised platform area where my father and the other council members stood.

I tried to catch Daddy's eye, but his face was serious and he seemed to look right through me. He stood next to the prophet's brother, Wade Barton, who looked as thick and solid as the brick incinerator out behind our house. His dark hair lay in a dense patch across his head, and his eyes were heavy-lidded like the geckos that ran and hid under the desert rocks. He rubbed his fingers against his palms as if he had an itch. Looking at him made me nervous.

We waited a long time and finally the prophet, Uncle Kenton, emerged and took his place before the crowd. Everyone fell silent, and I leaned forward, waiting to hear what he would say. He may be rather pudgy and pale, but Uncle Kenton has a powerful speaking voice that reaches right inside and you know he is talking directly to you. He can peer straight into our souls and read our hidden thoughts. He stared at us for a moment, taking in the hush that had fallen over the group, and then he began.

"You all know that the greatest duty a woman has is to her husband, to submit to his will, to his desire, and to his dominance. It is only through pleasing her husband that a woman may know God's grace. It is through the sacrament of plural marriage that she helps him attain his place in the celestial kingdom."

Beside me, my mother was nodding at the prophet's words. I thought of Joseph John and how our union would allow me to know God's grace.

"Without a husband-priesthood head to guide her in the path of righteousness, a woman is a wanton, dangerous, and wayward vessel. We have all learned from the examples of women in this community who have stepped off the path, narrow and straight, that leads to salvation. And I often think that we have weeded out this stain of evil that threatens the very foundation of our lives. But I am sorely proven wrong when I learn that the devil is alive and well within our community, working his sorcery against God's chosen people!"

A shudder went through the crowd. Satan was at work in Pineridge? Who had fallen into sin? Who had invited the destroyer inside the walls?

The prophet continued, his voice rising. "Just this morning, during the holy ritual of baptism of the dead, one of my brother's wives, Ann Marie Barton, a woman sanctified before the Lord in celestial marriage, tried to abandon our paradise here in Pineridge. She took advantage of the piety of this community to try and flee to a life of perdition and sin in the world of the Gentiles. She abandoned her duty to her husband, her children, and to God!" He spat these last words out like a poison, his eyes flashing at us.

Then Ann Marie Barton was led out by one of her sons and presented to the crowd. Sister Ann Marie was Brother Wade's fourth wife; I remember when they were married because Daddy gave them a fancy knitted blanket of good wool that Mama made. Sister Ann Marie kept her eyes on the floor. She had to be twenty-five now. Her hair was pulled into a loose bun at her neck and her pale eyes were red-rimmed when she finally looked up at us. It was in those eyes that I saw that this was no regular community gathering, it was something different.

I looked at Leigh Ann and she saw it too. I tried to pull back in my chair but I felt Sister Cora's assertive hand on my back.

The heat began to rise on my neck as the prophet continued. "I cannot tell you the pain and humiliation it causes me to see one of my own family fall into the devil's grasp. To see the shock and despair in my brother's eyes that one of his beloved wives, one of the tender souls he has taken into his heart and home, should betray him in this shameful way. I prayed and asked the Lord for guidance and I received a revelation. Ann Marie Barton, fourth wife of my brother Wade, is to be disciplined and punished before the families of our council, for her transgression. It is the Lord's will and desire that the community be witness to this evil being driven from her spirit at my brother's hand."

Sister Ann Marie broke into a loud wail and threw herself at the feet of the prophet, pleading for mercy. Uncle Kenton looked at her with no expression as he signaled for Brother Wade to come forward. My stomach tightened up into a knot when Sister Ann Marie stood to face her husband. The difference in size was terrifying. Wade Barton hulked and loomed over her as she stood motionless, her eyes closed, her lips moving in silent prayer. He raised a thick hand and brought the back of it against her cheek in a solid, swift blow. I flinched, wanting to look away, but I couldn't.

Sister Ann Marie was knocked off balance and stumbled, catching herself before falling, only to take a brutal kick from her husband. His eyes were blazing with uncontrolled fury. He grabbed her by the collar of her dress and held her up while he struck her repeatedly with his open hand. I was rooted to my chair in fear, unable to move. As each blow landed, Brother Wade grunted and groaned in rage. Sister Ann Marie's cheek split open and a spurt of blood shot out, but Brother Wade kept going, his hand slipping against the stickiness on her face. When she fell a second time, he pinned her face down with his knee in her back and delivered sharp swift blows to her rib cage. The crowd shifted uneasily but stayed in place, witnessing the prophet's revelation made flesh. I looked to my mother, who watched the terrifying spectacle with a look of grim satisfaction. I took Leigh Ann's arm and tried to turn away, but Sister Cora leaned in to block our way and hissed, "This is the price you pay for disobedience! Let it be a lesson to both of you!"

I wanted to cry but I was afraid that I would get in trouble so I stayed quiet, praying it would end soon.

Brother Wade pulled his wife onto her feet again. Her eyes were now swollen shut and her mouth was bleeding as he continued to strike and shake her. Her knees buckled underneath her and I saw a dark stain of urine pooling on the carpet beneath her. Then she fell in a heap on the ground, past the point of crying or making any sound at all. Brother Wade panted heavily, his shirt stained with his wife's blood and his own sweat. I sat on my hands to keep them from shaking, but I could feel my whole body trembling despite my efforts to stay calm.

Why doesn't anyone say something? Why doesn't someone do something? Why don't I?

I searched my father's face for any sign that would help me

make sense of what had just happened but I saw his gaze fixed on Brother Wade's fifteen-year-old daughter, Marcie, strikingly pretty in her pink cotton dress. Marcie's eyes drifted over Sister Ann Marie's limp body and caught Daddy's gaze. She smiled modestly and looked down.

My heart felt as if it would jump out of my chest for pounding so hard. The prophet stepped forward. His voice was calm, quiet. He smiled gently at us.

"We have witnessed the hand of righteousness defeat the scourge of the devil. My brother has driven the devil from Ann Marie, who is now before us as a new and humbled spirit, ready to accept the joys of serving God's will through celestial marriage. You may all go home now and think on this lesson."

We stood and left. There was little talk as we walked to our homes, such was the impact of bearing witness to the prophet's revelation carried out. I looked back to see Brother Wade carrying Sister Ann Marie away, her body like a rag doll in his powerful arms.

That evening I was unable to sleep. Every time I closed my eyes I saw Ann Marie Barton flailing and falling under Wade's fists, the blood spraying across the beige carpeting.

How could God have sanctioned such a savage beating? I knew it was a sin to question God's will or the divinity of the prophet, but I couldn't help feeling uneasy about what I had just witnessed. Was God to be found in Wade Barton's fury as he beat his wife senseless?

I could not calm my mind. I was troubled by questions that I could not answer, that I knew could be my damnation. I tossed fitfully in my bed and finally drifted into sleep. I awoke several hours later with a stab of pain in my lower abdomen. A cramp seized me and I made my way through the silent house to the bathroom.

Then I saw the dark red bloodstain on my sacred garments. The moment I had been waiting for had arrived, but I did not feel any of the joy I had anticipated. A cold dread rose from someplace deep inside me and settled over my heart. I looked at my reflection in the mirror. My cycle had begun. I was now a woman. I was ready to do God's work.

CHAPTER FIVE

THE SUN WAS SHINING, BRIGHT AND RELENTLESS, when I glanced at the clock on the kitchen wall; it was only seven o'clock in the morning and already the air was burning hot. I felt sick and exhausted with the arrival of my first menstrual cycle. My insides were wracked with a constant, dull ache that made me feel heavy and slow. I knew that the onset of bleeding was to be celebrated as it marked a young woman as ready to serve God, to be a jewel in her husband's heavenly crown, but I felt miserable and fidgety, with my stomach all out of sorts. I kept my head down as I turned out another half dozen loaves of bread from the oven, not wanting to attract any attention from my mother or the other sister wives.

I had been waiting for this day for so long but now that it was here, I felt uneasy. I had slept poorly to boot. The images of Ann Marie Barton's discipline had crept into my dreams. As much as I tried to push it away, the scene kept popping into my head, forcing its way into my consciousness. I focused on the activity in the busy kitchen: the sounds of the children running back and forth, Sister Cora cooking up breakfast. But Sister Ann Marie's face kept coming back and I could feel the defensive hunch of her slim shoulders as she prepared for each burst of her husband's fury.

Of course Sister Ann Marie had committed a grave sin by attempting to flee, but I wished Uncle Kenton in his infinite power had been able to cleanse her spirit without such violence. Shouldn't there have been another, gentler way? Thoughts like these had plagued me all night, and like Sister Ann Marie's face, they would not go away. I knew they were akin to blasphemy; no one questioned the prophet's revelations. I was all out of sorts; I couldn't even name what was bothering me so. And that made me as uncomfortable as the throbbing pain in my lower back.

"Alva Jane! Those loaves are getting too brown!" my mother admonished. "Where is your head today, girl?"

I reached in to retrieve the remaining loaves from the oven, burning my forearm on the hot oven door. "Sorry, Mama. I just didn't sleep too well."

"Well, I can see that. You've got dark circles under your eyes like a raccoon! Give me that arm." Mama took it and rubbed a cold slab of butter on the burn.

"I would think that you and Leigh Ann should have slept as soundly as two bugs in a rug, after being invited to the prophet's house last night. It's not often that young girls are allowed to attend such an important meeting," Sister Cora said, frying up a batch of scrambled eggs.

I exchanged a glance with Leigh Ann, who looked like she hadn't slept much either.

"What you two girls saw last night marked your entrance into the community as grown women," Mama agreed. "The prophet granted you the privilege of being in attendance so that you could see the seriousness of breaking the bonds of celestial marriage. We can only hope and pray that Ann Marie will now take up the cloak of righteousness and submission to her husband as her path to exaltation."

"Yes, Mama." I fought a wave of nausea that came over me.

Mama grabbed my chin and looked into my eyes. "Are you sick, Alva Jane? Do you have a fever?" She laid the back of her hand across my forehead.

"You're not bleeding are you?" Sister Cora asked.

"No, ma'am, not yet," I lied.

"You'd better be starting soon or you might have a condition."

"She has no condition, Sister Cora," Mama said sharply. "She's fourteen. Your Leigh Ann is a year older and she just started a few months ago."

"And wasn't I worried that her cycle came so late? You girls need to know that if you have something wrong with your cycle, you have no chance of fulfilling God's mission for you. Why do you think that Brenda Norton and her husband have no children? He's a fine-looking man and she's old enough to have several by now."

"Well, if she does have something wrong with her, then she's taking the right steps in joining the Brotherhood, giving her husband the opportunity to enter to the celestial kingdom through The Principle," Mama said.

I knew that once my mother and Sister Cora started like this they could go on forever, each one needing to have the last word, to be right. "I'm going to get ready for school," I said. I was anxious to leave the heat of the kitchen.

"Well, I don't want you lazing around here today, Alva Jane," Sister Cora said. "When you're done with school, I'm going to need your help with a special project."

"Yes, Sister Cora." I escaped up the stairs to fetch my books.

I walked to school with my usual group of sisters and cousins but I didn't take part in their talk and laughter. My mind kept going in circles over the same question again and again.

Why did I lie about my cycle?

I had never kept anything from my mother or my sisters. I looked at Liza, Laura Jean, Carlene, and Olive, and felt the urge to blurt out my good news, but something inside held me back. It seemed that today nothing was as it should be. I had sneaked an extra pad from Leigh Ann's box and hidden it in my book bag, along with some sewing patterns for Brenda Norton. I would tell my sister about the pad after dinner. I would tell them all and then I would feel better.

Outside the Zion Academy I saw Joseph John arriving for the morning class with his younger brother, Abel. I may have kept my cycle a secret from my family but I knew that today I would find the right time to tell him. The arrival of my cycle meant that we could be married and that thought pushed back all the discomfort I had felt since waking up. He smiled at me and I wondered if he could see anything different about me today.

Inside, the hymns that usually were piped in over the PA system had been replaced. Instead, we heard the voice of the prophet, recorded from a sermon on the laws of celestial marriage.

"The only true freedom of women is in the following the Celestial law of plural marriage and submitting herself to her husband's dominion and living his law. There is no force in this. The prophet doesn't force you to heaven; it is your own pure and willing spirit. And when you enter into marriage, you do not have the right to think that you have been forced. You know it will be your choice when you speak the vows. Because the judgments are coming very soon and the only way to survive is to keep sweet and follow God's law. . . .

Sometimes the prophet would insist that his sermons be played at school and in other gathering places in Pineridge. It was usually when there was a weakness among us, a faltering of faith as Mama called it, and his words were a boon and a balm, to help to keep us strong. In the recreation area outside, Sister Emily was directing a group of younger children who carried books and dumped them onto a pile. I saw my brother Cliff watching, his long frame leaning against the doorway.

If Cliff had been my age, we could be twins. We have the same hair and eyes, the same long arms and legs that get in the way of everything. He wore a heavy denim shirt a half size too small; it made him look younger than his seventeen years. I saw that look in his eyes and knew that he would not hold his tongue but before I could caution him, he blurted out, "What are they doing with the books, Sister Emily?"

"The prophet has ordered all writings here at school other than his own to be destroyed."

"Why? All we read are FLDS books anyway. We don't even get to read made-up stories."

I knew he was pushing to see how far he could go. Why did he have to be like that? Sister Emily looked about ready to give him a wallop but she just said, "The prophet knows what is best and his judgment is not to be questioned. We are only going to have the prophet's own writings here in the academy. My brother Kenton received it in a revelation from God last night."

Sister Emily stressed the words "my brother" to remind us that she was the sister of the prophet and not to be crossed. My heart pounded in fear for Cliff. Everyone knew that you did not question a revelation or decree from the prophet. Cliff's eyes had a hard, rebellious set to them as he faced off with Sister Emily and I had to do something to stop this from going any further. I walked to him and took his arm, leading him away.

"Don't provoke her, Cliff. What does it matter to you if they have a silly old book or not? What if she tells the prophet what you said?"

"And what did I say? That we don't get to read anything but FLDS stuff anyway? Not everyone is this way, Alva. There's a whole big world out there and they don't live like we do."

"I know that, but we don't want to live that way, do we, Cliff? Those people are lost, their souls will never get to the celestial kingdom. We're God's chosen people, don't forget that."

"Other kids read made-up stories, just for fun. . . ." Cliff's voice trailed off. I could see that he was angry and confused all at the same time.

Then he walked away from me, without another word, to join the Paine brothers. I watched him go; he had clearly been spending too much time with the wrong group of people lately. Since he had started hanging out with Jimmy and Elias Paine, Cliff had started to go bad. There was even talk that he had been seen in town with Tara, the younger sister of those Paine boys. How she had the nerve to go into town at all, let alone be seen with a boy, amazed me. Their mama had died in a car wreck out in Nevada two years ago while doing missionary work and the other sister wives didn't take much care of them anymore.

They were straying and now Cliff had become part of their group and he was starting to quarrel over all kinds of things, asking questions, disagreeing even with Daddy. Just last week I'd overheard my father and Cliff arguing about his upcoming mission, something that all the boys are required to do when they are old enough. Mama had ordered all the children out of the house so we wouldn't hear, but I was still on the front porch when Cliff raised his voice to Daddy and said, "I know how it works. You'll send me off for two years and when I come back from some godforsaken place, Tara will be married off to an old man who will set her on the straight and narrow path!"

For that insolence, Cliff had received a sharp slap across the face and I'd seen the red welt on his cheek when he'd run from the house, wiping his eyes. But he hadn't learned his lesson. He was starting more trouble now with Sister Emily and it was leading him down a dangerous road.

Joseph John walked by and gave me a sweet, sympathetic look. Then Cliff's words echoed in my head: *There's a whole big world out there.*

Cliff was right. There was indeed a whole big world out there and soon Joseph John would be living in it, facing temptation at every turn. I knew I had to tell him as soon as possible about my cycle. I had to get my marriage sealed and settled. I knew I could not bear the anxiety of wondering who Joseph John might be meeting at BYU while I was stuck here in Pineridge, baking bread.

I had just settled into my seat in the schoolroom when Sister Emily doused the pile of books with gasoline and tossed a lit match onto it. As the flames crackled and rose, the acrid smoke wafted through the open window, stinging my eyes. I put my forehead against the cool, worn wood of my desk. Somehow this day was going from bad to worse and I couldn't name why.

I hurried home, long after school had ended, the sewing patterns for Brenda Norton still in my bag. There had been no time to drop them off. Sister Emily had made me stay after school to wash down all the desks and chalkboards. It was my punishment for having fallen asleep while she read from volume eighteen of the Journal of Discourses, reciting the speeches of the early Mormon leaders.

As I ran up the front porch I heard my mother's voice. "Cliff is just acting like a boy, Emily. They all go through that rebellious phase. There's no need to make it more than it is."

"He has been stirring up the other students, asking questions he shouldn't be, and challenging authority," Sister Emily snapped back. Just as I feared, Sister Emily had come home with word of Cliff's behavior and now Daddy would hear of it.

I came into the kitchen to find my mother and the other sister wives at work canning the summer vegetables from the garden. "Why are you late, Alva Jane?" Sister Cora asked. "You weren't visiting with that Joseph John Hilliard, were you?"

I felt my face turn hot with embarrassment. "Of course not, Sister Cora. I hardly ever see him; he goes to the public school. Sister Emily asked me to stay late to clean up the schoolroom."

"Good. Nothing good can come of young girls fraternizing with boys. You've heard it from the prophet a hundred times: Boys are snakes; they are not to be trusted. All they want is to take your virtue. They will not lead you to be exalted in the eyes of the Lord, but cast down."

"Amen," agreed Sister Emily.

I nodded, anxious to get off this subject. "You said you had some special chores for me today, Sister Cora?"

"Yes, I want you to go to my brother Wade's house and help take care of Sister Ann Marie. She is recovering from the discipline last night, and although her sprit is undoubtedly strengthened, her body is in need of healing."

To Wade Barton's house? To help take care of Sister Ann Marie, whose image haunted me all night?

That was the last place I wanted to go. I looked to my mother, hoping she would insist that I had chores to do at home or in the yard, anyplace besides Wade Barton's house. But Mama was busy with the canning, her face damp from the steam rising from boiling the canning jars. She did not look up and I knew she would not take my part in this or go against Sister Cora when Cliff was causing problems. This was part of the constant shift and struggle for influence that infused our family life, the jockeying for position among the sister wives. If a child was disobedient or causing trouble, it was a reflection of the mother's failings; her status and her power were diminished. My mother could not rescue me. I had no choice but to agree to Sister Cora's request.

"Of course, Sister Cora. Once I change to my work dress I'll be ready to go."

I headed for the stairs and heard Sister Cora's voice behind me. "That's a good girl, Alva Jane. You keep sweet like that and you'll make a fine wife to a lucky man."

Keep sweet. Those were the words that all of us girls lived by in Pineridge. They were cross-stitched onto the pillow Mama gave me for my last birthday, and they hung above the kitchen doorway as a framed embroidery sampler. *Keep sweet* reminds us that obedience with a willing and happy heart is our main requirement before God. And I would keep sweet, no matter what I had to face. I would do what God required of me and I would be rewarded with a celestial marriage for all eternity to the boy I loved.

I felt a stab of cramping as I reached into the strongbox

stowed under Leigh Ann's bed. I grabbed two more sanitary pads and was tucking them into the folds of my dress when I heard Leigh Ann giggle behind me.

"I knew it!" she said, kneeling next to me. "I keep count of how many pads I have and I knew two went missing! When did you get it?"

"Just last night, but I haven't told anyone yet. Please keep quiet about it, Leigh Ann. There's been so much going on with Cliff. I want to wait until the right time to tell Mama."

"Sure. It can just be our secret. You know what this means, don't you? They're going to be finding husbands for us soon!"

I smiled, keeping my plans with Joseph John to myself. "I've got to go. Sister Cora is sending me over to Wade Barton's house to take care of Sister Ann Marie."

"Let me know if you want some female tea when you get back. I know how to make it; my mama showed me last month," Leigh Ann offered.

"Thanks, and keep it a secret, promise?"

"Promise."

We linked our pinkie fingers and tugged.

I walked slowly toward Wade Barton's house. I hoped to meet Joseph John returning from school or chores. I had to find a moment to tell him that we could finally ask for permission to be married. But he was nowhere to be seen.

I arrived at Brother Wade's house. Its wood and white paint had suffered beneath the harsh desert sun, unlike the prophet's limestone compound, which stood like a fortress against the elements. I knocked on the door, trying to keep my mind steady, fighting off the fear I felt.

What condition will Sister Ann Marie be in after yesterday's events? Why can't her other sister wives take care of her, as is their duty?

Sister LeNan, Brother Wade's fifth wife, opened the door. She had left school at thirteen to prepare for marriage to the prophet's brother. Sister LeNan had to be eighteen now and her belly was swollen with her third child. She stepped aside to welcome me in.

"Oh, hi there, Alva Jane. It's so nice to see you again. Sister Cora told Wade that you'd be coming over to help with Ann Marie." She had the same singsong voice I remembered from when we were in school together.

I followed her into the living room. All the curtains were drawn against the heat. The floors gleamed; there was not a speck of dust anywhere. Framed images of all the prophets throughout history hung on the walls, staring at us in mute judgment. Everything was in its place but there was a stillness to it that made me uncomfortable. It was so different from my own house, which bustled with kids and the bickering among the sister wives. Here, the silence hung like a veil.

"Are your sister wives out?" I asked.

"Oh, no. They're here, working. Our husband likes quiet, all the time. Says he doesn't like the chattering of women and children, like a bunch of magpies!"

"Where are the children?"

"The big boys are out back, the girls are helping us with the chores, and the smallest are in the attic. They can play up there without making much noise."

We stood, looking at each other, unsure of what to say next.

"When is your baby due?" I finally asked.

"Oh, in a few weeks, but Lord, I feel so swollen I'd swear it will be any day now! I'm just so big and I feel so tired all the time it's hard to do my daily chores. Sister Irene has us on a tight schedule around here. Mondays we clean the bedrooms and linens, wash the walls and all the upstairs windows. Tuesdays we do the floors, scrubbing and waxing. Wednesdays it's kitchen top to bottom, disinfecting everything. Sister Irene, Wade's first wife, is very tough on germs. . . ." Sister LeNan rattled on, while I nodded.

"That's a lot of work to do. But you only have one month to go until the baby comes," I said.

"I know, it's not long. My last one, Charlene, was five weeks early. I sure wish this one would come early too! But what I'm really hoping for is a Down's baby," Sister LeNan whispered with a giggle.

I had heard of other women hoping for a child with Down's syndrome or some other problem. Most sister wives depend on government help and food stamps to feed their children, and having a Down's baby means more aid. A handicapped child is a blessing and gift from God for this reason. Before I could say anything, I heard Wade Barton's heavy step on the floorboards and turned to see him standing in the doorway.

Up close his body seemed even bigger and thicker than I

remembered from the previous night. His neck joined his sloping shoulders as one bulky mass of muscle; his forehead was low and jutted out, giving him the look of an angry animal. He stared at me for a long moment and I was so nervous I didn't dare speak or know where to put my hands.

"Welcome to our home, Alva Jane. My sister suggested that you come to help my wife Ann Marie. Said you are very good with healing," he said finally.

"Thank you for having me, Mr. Barton. Anything I can do to help . . ." My voice sounded so small that I thought better of it and just fell quiet.

"Follow me." He turned toward the kitchen.

We walked to a steep staircase at the back of the kitchen and down to the basement, which had been converted into a windowless room. There I saw Sister Ann Marie, propped up on a pile of pillows in a bed covered with a faded patchwork quilt. Her face was bruised and misshapen, the right side of it immobile from the swelling. One of her eyes was covered with an oozing bandage. She wore a loose nightgown and I could see raised red marks on her neck. She didn't look at me, keeping her one eye trained on her husband where he stood at the side of the bed.

"I had to take her in to the doctor in town this morning, had to wire that jaw shut. She can't talk much and she can only drink through a straw but she's quiet. She needs to have those bandages changed and to be given liquids; that's what the doctor said."

I wondered if the doctor in town had been at all curious

about the cause of the injuries. As if he could read my mind, Brother Wade said, "He's good FLDS, he didn't ask any questions. I told him she'd smashed the car, trying to learn to drive— something women shouldn't undertake, and he agreed!"

Then he laughed, a dry scratchy sound that reminded me of a barking dog. I smiled and hoped he would leave, so I set about preparing Sister Ann Marie's bandages, pouring some fresh water into her glass.

"She likes it when you read to her," Brother Wade said, gesturing toward the table, where he had placed several pamphlets on plural marriage that Uncle Kenton had written, along with a copy of the Doctrines and Covenants. "Good to reinforce right thinking in her mind now that her body's had the devil driven out."

"Yes, sir."

"My first wife, Irene, doesn't take to any lollygagging around the house. The other sister wives all have duties to perform. None can spare the time to be down here with Ann Marie, especially now that they have to make up for her work too. I'll thank my sister Cora for sending you over, Alva Jane. Much appreciated."

Once he was gone, I turned to Sister Ann Marie. "Can I put a new gauze on?"

She nodded and I pulled the wet gauze from her face. Beneath it, her bad eye was swollen shut and weeping fluid. It looked so beyond repair that I didn't think she would ever see out of it again. I applied a fresh bandage to it, trying not to hurt her, but she flinched when the new cotton gauze touched her

MICHELE DOMINGUEZ GREENE

raw skin. Then I sat back, unsure what to do next. Ann Marie seemed to relax a little as she turned her good eye to me. She grunted and mumbled things I could not understand through her wired jaw.

"Do you want water? Juice?" I asked.

She shook her head slowly and drew a sharp intake of breath in response to pain somewhere in her bruised body.

"I can read to you if you'd like," I offered. I opened the book of Doctrines and Covenants. Sister Ann Marie shook her head again and I could feel her distress.

"What would you like me to do?"

She moved one of her bandaged hands out from under the quilt, three fingers set in a splint. She slid her arm stiffly toward the edge of the bed. Her small hand lay there like a fish that had been pulled from the water and given up the battle to breathe. The effort had cost her and she closed her eyes, exhausted. She looked so awful and I felt so sorry for her that I reached my hand out and laid it over hers, careful not to hurt the broken fingers. She took in a surprised breath when she felt my touch. A moment later, the eye bandage was wet and weeping fluid again. It was only when I removed it that I saw that it was not damp with pus but with Sister Ann Marie's tears. She cried silently, and her suffering seemed so deep it made me feel like she was locked in a room that I could not enter even if I tried.

I hoped she would fall asleep and stay that way. I wanted to get out of the Barton house, to run to the safety and routine of my own home and not look back. My cramps had subsided and I could feel my blood flowing freely now; the pad between my legs was heavy and damp. Ann Marie's eyes remained closed; her ragged breathing became steady as she drifted into sleep. I sat, watching her for a long time, afraid to move.

CHAPTER SIX

FOR SIX DAYS SISTER CORA INSISTED THAT I HELP TAKE care of Ann Marie. Each day when I returned home I felt relieved, like I had passed through a dark and dangerous place unscathed. Sister Cora could not fault me for anything; I had done what was asked of me willingly. I had kept sweet. Soon I would be allowed to return to school and my job at the Pineridge store.

I had just returned from the Barton house and was coming up the front porch when I heard my father's voice from the living room. He was not usually home at this hour. I knew something important was happening when I came in and saw Daddy, Mama, and all the other sister wives assembled together.

"Hi, Daddy," I said, but he gave me nothing more than a quick nod. I was hurt but did my best to hide my feelings beneath a smile.

"Go on up to your room, Alva. We've got some family business to discuss," my mother said.

I obeyed and headed up the staircase but hovered at the top step, listening. Leigh Ann stepped out of her room and joined me.

"What's going on?" I mouthed.

Leigh Ann leaned in and whispered in my ear. "Sister Emily went to the prophet to complain about Cliff. I guess it was not the first time she spoke to him about it. Now he's called Daddy in for a meeting."

I felt suddenly cold. Uncle Kenton was calling Daddy in for a meeting? That was serious, and I didn't want to think of what the outcome might be. Leigh Ann put her finger to her lips and we waited, hoping to catch a snippet of conversation from below. All we heard at first were the soft voices of the women murmuring among themselves. Then Daddy's forceful voice rose above the rest.

"I don't know what possessed you, Emily. This is a family matter; we could have handled it among ourselves. The boy is getting out of line, but I could have taken steps to deal with that. I was already talking about sending him to Short Creek for a reform retreat. Now it may be out of my hands."

Sister Emily's nasal voice pitched higher than usual in consternation. "I just felt I had to do something, Eldon Ray. He's stirring up insubordination among the others at school."

Then my mother said, "Sister Emily went to the prophet to make problems for me and my children. She wants to paint us as troublemakers because of her own jealousies!"

"I did nothing of the sort. She—" Sister Emily shot back but Daddy cut her off.

"I will not have this backbiting and carrying on under my roof! The prophet has called a meeting with me because he thinks I cannot control my own family and at moments like these, you women prove him right! There is indeed jealousy among you and when it strikes, love requires an hour on your knees praying alone and asking for forgiveness and the resurrection of peace in our home. Emily, you will think twice before you go behind my back to your brother again, if you know what's good for you. Just like a woman, you have no sense or idea what you could be bringing down upon this family."

It was the first time I had ever heard my father speak that way. Leigh Ann and I hurried to our rooms when we heard him rise, his footsteps coming toward the foyer. A moment later Mama stepped into our bedroom and closed the door.

"She did it on purpose, just to get us in trouble, no matter what she says!" she whispered fiercely. "I warned Cliff that something like this could happen with Cora and Emily always looking for some way to bring us down!"

"What do you think Uncle Kenton will do, Mama?"

"I don't know, honey. Your father is a faithful servant to the prophet, Uncle Kenton's right hand. But you just never know. . . ." Her voice trailed off and she took a kitchen timer from her dresser drawer. She set it at one hour. Then she knelt at the edge of her bed, bowed her head, and began praying, as my father had ordered her to.

Clearly now was not the time to tell Mama about my cycle.

Daddy went to the prophet's compound after dinner and when he returned, he went straight upstairs to Sister Cora's room, leaving the rest of us to wonder what had happened. The whole house was in a state of uncertainty but we could do nothing but wait for some word from Daddy.

I stayed up well past dinnertime and scripture reading, cleaning the kitchen shelves and reorganizing the cookware in hopes of talking to Cliff when he got home but he had still not returned when Mama told me it was time for bed.

I waited under my covers, staring at the ceiling in the dark of our room until I heard the even breathing of my sisters and my mother. Then I walked quietly down to the kitchen with my math book to work on my sums and wait up for Cliff. It was close to midnight when I heard his gentle push at the kitchen door and he stepped into the dim light, his handsome face in half shadow.

"Where have you been? There's a heap of trouble about you, Cliff."

"I was over visiting the Paine boys," he said, settling into a chair.

"Sister Emily went to the prophet and complained about your behavior."

"Sister Emily complains about everything," Cliff replied.

"And Uncle Kenton called Daddy in for a meeting to discuss it."

Now Cliff sat up. "A meeting? When was it?"

"Earlier this evening. Daddy was nervous. He called a gathering of all the sister wives first and I heard him tell Sister Emily that she did not know what kind of trouble she was bringing down upon the family."

"Did he say what happened?"

Now Cliff's defiance had disappeared; he looked as frightened as I was.

"He didn't. He came in and went straight to Sister Cora's room, didn't even come down for evening scripture reading."

Cliff stared straight through me. After a long silence, he asked, "What do you think will happen, Alva?"

"Daddy said he was thinking of sending you to the reform retreat at Short Creek."

Cliff grimaced. Short Creek is another FLDS community in Arizona, at the southern border with Utah. The reform retreat entails hours of hard manual labor and living with a devout FLDS family, reciting scripture, and reading and studying the Doctrines and Covenants, until the offender is brought to heel and his rebellion subdued. I knew several boys in Pineridge who had been sent there. Otis Ewell was one and he had been forced to sleep in the car of his host family and had only been given one meal a day. Otis had eventually run off and was never seen again. I hoped Cliff would fare better with the Crickers.

I looked at the worn cotton tablecloth with the faded sunflower design, the chipped sugar bowl, and a slab of fresh butter on a blue china plate, ready for tomorrow's breakfast. These were the familiar things that I saw every day, that were part of my daily life. My brother's presence was like that, passing each other on the stairway, sitting across the dinner table. I would miss him terribly if he were sent to the Crickers but maybe it would be best for him.

"If you do get sent to Short Creek, you're going to have to stay on the straight and narrow path, Cliff. You can't be sneaking off to town or any of the other stuff you've been doing."

"I'm not going to Short Creek, Alva. Daddy was bluffing, he wouldn't send me there."

"It's not up to Daddy anymore."

"We've never had any trouble with Uncle Kenton," Cliff said. His words were optimistic but his voice came out thin and reedy. I could tell he was scared. "Heck, Cora and Emily are his sisters. Short Creek? Never going to happen, Alva. Trust me."

I just stared at him in the yellow light of the milk glass lamp on the kitchen counter. I hoped he was right.

I awoke early, eager to find out about Cliff's fate. My menstrual cramps had subsided but the blood continued to flow. I would need to get a steady supply of pads before the day was out. Which meant I really needed to tell Mama soon, even if she did have other things on her mind. After bathing, I went down to help in the kitchen.

The moment I saw my mother's face, I knew something bad had happened. I could not remember the last time I had seen Mama cry but today her eyes were red and swollen. There was a palpable tension in the air and Sister Cora and Sister Emily kept busy preparing breakfast. I took up my work next to Mama, kneading and pounding the dough.

"What's going on, Mama?" I whispered.

Mama wiped her eyes with the back of her hand but she spoke in a clear, steady voice. "Your brother Cliff is leaving the community today. We'll be driving him out to the highway after we finish up with breakfast."

My brother is leaving the community?

"When will he be back? Where's he going?"

"He won't be back, Alva Jane. The prophet has expelled him from Pineridge and the Brotherhood of the Lord," Mama said, turning back to her work.

Expelled? Never coming back?

It couldn't be true! Cliff had never lived anywhere but Pineridge; he had no idea how to get by in the outside world. I knew I should hold my tongue in front of Sister Cora and Sister Emily but I couldn't.

"Can't Daddy convince Uncle Kenton not to do it?"

"No one convinces the prophet of anything, Alva, you know that. His decisions are based on revelation from God. And this is what God told him to do with Cliff."

Mama moved to get more flour from the pantry, making it clear to me that the discussion was over. Cliff was leaving. It couldn't be true, but it was. I tried to concentrate on the bread making but I could feel tears rising behind my eyes.

I knew several boys who had been expelled; it seemed that every year there were one or two who caught Uncle Kenton's attention and were labeled a threat to the community. Some of the lesser families had seen their sons go, but this was the first time I had heard of a council member's family being punished this way.

I could not imagine my brother gone from our lives. He had been asleep in the next room every night since I was born. He had been out in the yard chopping up wood or pulling mustard greens, his full-throated laugh had filled the living room on countless nights as he teased the girls or wrestled the younger boys.

He was Mama's firstborn and I knew his departure was going to be a hard and bitter pill for her to swallow. But I also knew that Mama would not protest. Her faith was as deep as the earth below the Hill Cumorah where the angel Moroni revealed the secret golden plates to Joseph Smith. Mama accepted the prophet's word as God's will. There would be no remedy. Cliff would leave Pineridge.

I heard my father's footsteps on the stairway. He paused in the doorway. "Uncle Kenton has called me to drive him to a meeting with some real estate people in town. I'll be heading over to his compound in a moment," he said.

This was his way of letting us know that he would not be there to take Cliff out to the highway and say good-bye. I suddenly felt angry.

How can he let this happen? And how can he not say good-bye to his own son?

He was our father, the ruler and rock of our family. But it would be Mama and the rest of us who had to face the hard task of letting Cliff go. My stomach felt all topsy-turvy, like a mixing blender gone awry. I never got angry with my parents, least of all Daddy. I was not keeping sweet and I knew that God would be disappointed in me but I didn't know how else to feel. Things like this just didn't happen in our family. I kept hoping Daddy would tell us it had been a mistake, that he would make things right. But he didn't. He ate his breakfast in silence and left.

An hour later, I sat behind my mother, who was at the wheel of the old Chevy Impala that Daddy had given to his primary wives. My younger siblings and I were piled into the backseat, a jumble of arms and legs, our dusty shoes scuffing up against one another's shins. Ten-year-old Liza held the baby, Rowena, on her lap and Olive bounced three-year-old Marcus on her knees to keep him quiet. He was unsettled, like all of us, especially the eight-year-old twins, Lucas and Leon, who looked up to Cliff like a second father.

In the passenger seat, Cliff sat stiffly, a small duffel bag on his lap, his eyes glued to the road. No one spoke. It had all happened so quickly, we were in a state of shock. I had been forbidden to talk to Cliff since Mama had told me of the prophet's decree. I had been unable to help him pack his clothes, to decide what keepsakes to take, to give him the shiny piece of rose quartz he had helped me dig up years before, out by the red rock ridge. He had been left alone in his room to prepare for his new life.

Mama maneuvered the car through the streets of Pineridge until we reached the main guard gate and towers where we pulled onto the highway. Daddy had instructed Mama to leave Cliff several miles from town, so as not to elicit any inquiries from strangers passing by. Boys who had been expelled were called Lost Boys. Some had gained attention from local press and others who took pity on them. Last year a reporter from Salt

Lake had come to the guard gates trying to get into Pineridge to talk to people about the Lost Boys, but he hadn't been allowed inside. But we all knew to be careful. Leaving Cliff too close to Pineridge might alert some passerby and Daddy didn't want anyone asking any questions about a boy alone out on the highway so close to the compound.

The car rumbled, dragging our heavy load of human sorrow down the empty highway, the desert spreading out endlessly all around us. A few miles from town, Mama pulled over and kept the engine running.

"You take care, son. Remember what you've learned, stay to the straight and narrow path." Mama pressed a small wad of bills into his hand, adding, "I've been saving this for a rainy day and I think this qualifies."

When Cliff spoke, his voice was thick. "I'll be okay, Mama. Don't you worry about me." He turned to face us and I saw panic in his eyes underneath his mask of bravado. "You all be good and mind Mama, do as she says and don't give her any trouble, you hear?"

Olive broke into sobs and reached for him. "Where are you going to go, Cliff? Where are you going to live?"

"I'll find my way. Don't you girls worry."

He reached out and mussed up Leon's curly hair. "And you two be big boys now. Don't be crying like your sisters."

I could see that Cliff was about to cry himself and I leaned forward to embrace him. When I put my arms around his slender shoulders, my tears broke free, wetting his faded denim shirt that I had mended countless times. I wanted to say something but no words came. I wanted to scream that this was wrong, this could not be happening to us, but I knew it was pointless. There was no turning back from this moment.

Cliff pushed the door open and stepped out, the morning sun lighting up his handsome face. He had inherited Mama's fine features, and our father's height and physical grace. I wondered for a moment if it might be true, what some of the rowdy boys whispered, that the prophet always managed to expel the handsomest boys, the ones who caught the attention of the young girls and became rivals to the older men in the community. Could that be why Uncle Kenton had taken such a hard stance against Cliff, why a trip to the Short Creek reform retreat was not enough to satisfy him?

I knew that the prophet was not motivated by such petty concerns, and that it was not my place to question revelations from God, but somewhere inside me, the question lingered. My faith was being tested, and it was up to me to prove it strong and true. It was easy to believe when everything was good. But when bad things happened, doubt sowed its seed in fertile soil and burrowed deep. It was my duty to root it out.

We watched Cliff walk down the highway, his pack slung over his shoulder. He looked so small and defenseless against the landscape. Lucas and Leon ignored his words and cried inconsolably. Mama turned the car around for the trip home and I could see that her cheeks were wet with silent tears. All of us pressed our faces against the back window, waving, trying to keep Cliff in our sights as long as we could until he was just a little speck on the highway.

On the way back, I vowed to do everything I could to keep sweet and follow my mother's example. Surely if I worked extra hard and demonstrated my obedience, then the nagging questions inside me would disappear and everything would return to normal. Ann Marie Barton would recover and be happy in her home life. I would be married to Joseph John and perhaps someday Cliff would even be allowed to come back. I repeated those words over and over in my head, willing them to come true.

As we neared Pineridge, Mama pulled over and turned to us, her tears now dry. "I don't want any of you to mention this to anyone or to talk of it at home, you understand? You are not to mention Cliff. Your brother is dead to you and to this family now. Once someone is expelled from the Brotherhood, he does not exist in the eyes of God; he has become an apostate. You must all be strong. Do not let the other sister wives see you crying or showing them any other sign of weakness. You are God's chosen children and your father's favorites, and that is all that matters."

We stared back at her in obedient silence; not one of us dared to speak a word. I felt the sinking certainty that nothing would return to normal ever again. Mama shifted the car into gear and guided it down the remaining highway, turning to pass the guard gates and towers, leading us back to the safety and security of home.

CHAPTER SEVEN

THE NEXT DAY, I WAS PREPARING MY BOOKS TO GO to school when Sister Cora stopped me.

"My brother Wade is so pleased with your help, Alva Jane, that he wants you to continue to come by every day to help with Ann Marie. He thinks you are a good influence on her."

"But I have to go back to school and I'm due to work with Mr. Battle at the store," I protested.

What I didn't say was that if I was kept out of school any longer, I'd have little chance to see Joseph John, let alone speak to him. My cycle had ended now and I still hadn't been able to let him know I was ready for marriage. I looked over at Mama, hoping she might intervene in my defense, but she busied herself with polishing the breakfront, removing the candlesticks for dusting. She did not speak up to support me. I knew she was unwilling to cause any more trouble since Cliff's expulsion.

"Your father has already called Mr. Battle to ask you to be dismissed from your duties while helping my brother. And Sister Emily says you are far ahead of the other girls in your schoolwork. Missing a few weeks won't set you back." Sister Cora's face was smug. She clearly savored my mother's silence.

"But I . . ." I had to say something but I didn't know what.

"But what, Alva Jane? Don't you realize what an honor it is to be asked to attend to the family of Uncle Kenton's brother? Wade is next in line to the prophet. Don't you think that this will be a boon to our family, especially after your brother's disgrace?" She couldn't resist turning the knife when the wound of Cliff's absence was still fresh.

"Of course, Sister Cora. I'm more than happy to go help with Sister Ann Marie."

"That's a good girl. When you return, I'll need you to gather some mustard greens out beyond the back fence for dinner."

These days she had no end of tasks for me, it seemed.

At Wade Barton's house I found Sister Ann Marie in much the same condition as the previous day. The air in the room was stale and smelled of sweat, salve, and bloody bandages discarded in the wastebasket. The broken blood vessel in her open eye had cleared a bit and I saw a flicker of recognition in it as I settled down next to her.

"How are you today?" I asked, knowing full well she could not really reply.

Sister Ann Marie nodded weakly and tried to speak but her words were unintelligible with her jaw wired shut.

"Don't you wear yourself out trying to talk. I can sit here and keep you company or tend to your bandages, whatever you need."

I read from the Doctrines and Covenants until she turned her face away from me, closing her unbandaged eye. I waited, unable to tell if she was asleep or just resting. The water pitcher was almost empty and the bandages were running low so I went upstairs to ask Sister Irene for more. In the hallway outside the kitchen, I saw Sister Cora's familiar brown purse on the break-front. Why was Sister Cora here? I paused before the door to the kitchen and heard her voice, in discussion with Sister Irene. I couldn't believe what she was saying.

"Alva Jane is a wonderful girl, so smart and industrious. I hate to say it but she's better than my Leigh Ann at her sewing and she's an excellent cook as well."

"She seems to have a calming influence on Ann Marie," Sister Irene said.

"She's a good girl and quite pretty, too."

I couldn't imagine what had come over Sister Cora to say such nice things about me when she was always finding fault with me at home. Maybe she was getting past her jealousies of my mother? Maybe my coming here every day to take care of her brother's wife made her feel more kindly toward me? Whatever it was, I was glad that she was being nice for a change. Maybe she could ask Brother Wade to let me return to school soon. I knew better than to interrupt their conversation, so I filled the water pitcher from the bathroom tap and slipped back downstairs.

Sister Ann Marie fell into a deep sleep in the early afternoon and Sister Irene let me leave to take the sewing patterns to Brenda Norton, so I could finally show her how to sew up a proper dress. I felt good being out of the Barton house and under the vast expanse of blue, cloudless sky.

When I arrived at Brenda's house, I saw her through the window before I reached the doorstep. She looked upset, wiping her eyes on her sleeve. I was about to leave when she spotted me and waved. The front door opened and she called out to me, "Alva Jane! Come on in, it's so nice to see you!"

I walked up the front porch and past her into the house. Right away I noticed the changes. Brenda had put a fresh coat of pale peach paint on the walls and hung pretty sheers in the front windows.

Brenda was dressed in the strangest outfit, a long skirt made of rough muslin and a high-necked blouse that was too big for her. I resolved to help her set up her sewing machine that very day and get started on some more attractive dresses.

"Can I get you some lemonade?" Brenda offered. Her voice was cheery, but the red in her eyes confirmed she'd been crying.

"Yes, thank you. I thought you might be needing them so I brought you these sewing patterns," I said.

"Oh, thank you! As you can see, I've borrowed some clothes from one of the neighbors and they don't fit too well."

I raised my eyebrows in agreement and something in that made Brenda laugh as she poured two glasses of lemonade.

"I guess I look pretty awful, huh? Jack insisted that I stop dressing in my work clothes when I am at home."

I figured that meant she still had her job at the bank. "How long do you think you'll stay on there?"

"As long as they'll have me. Jack is donating all of his time to help the prophet with the plans for the new community out in Arizona, so there's no money coming in except my salary."

That made sense, but I was amazed Brenda managed going every day from Pineridge to the outside world with all of its evil and temptation. "Isn't it hard? To go back and forth from your work to your life here?"

"A little. I like my job, so I feel good when I'm at the office. Here in Pineridge, I have a lot to learn and it's a little over-whelming sometimes. Plus, I'm alone so much here. Jack is always meeting with the council and I haven't had many visi-tors."

I knew why the other women hadn't warmed up to her. She was an outsider, and it would take a long time of her liv-ing The Principle before she was accepted as one of us. I didn't say anything as I didn't want to make her feel worse than she already did, judging from the way her eyes had gotten all shiny and damp.

Brenda stared into her glass of lemonade and then surprised me by asking, "What happens to a woman here in Pineridge if she's unable to have children?"

I thought of Sister Sherrie, who had only Orton, and Rita Mae, who had so few children. I had never known a woman who had none but I guessed there must have been some. "Well,

I don't know. I guess she would have a hard time being exalted if she couldn't do her duty to the Lord."

"Do the sister wives share their children among each other? Can a wife who has none of her own still be like a mother to them?"

I realized then that she was asking about herself. So it was true what Sister Cora had said. Brenda had no children yet because she was unable to. And I knew that must be why she was crying into her sleeve when I arrived. Now I felt bad for having been suspicious of her, even if she did have a can of Coca-Cola hidden away. Poor Brenda! She had no way to fulfill God's plan for her, no way to help her husband to build his kingdom, to be a jewel in his heavenly crown. She must have felt so useless and unworthy. I patted her arm.

"Once you have a few sister wives, your house will be so busy and full of children you won't know which end is up!"

This made Brenda cry openly. "Oh, I hope so! That's why I followed Jack here. He wants a family so badly and it's been six years we've been trying. He tells me now we'll have the family we've always wanted and I have to believe him, I guess. . . ."

She seemed so upset, I wanted to cheer her up, to make her feel useful, so I said, "I think you've done a lot with the house, Brenda. It looks a whole lot better than it did when Mitch DeLory was here."

"I'm just curious, Alva. What happened to the family that lived here before us? Your father just said that they left the community, but that seems to be a rare occurrence here in Pineridge. Where did they go?"

91

Brenda always seemed to ask me hard questions, ones that I had to think about before answering. We weren't supposed to talk about Mitch DeLory now that he was an apostate, the same way we weren't supposed to mention Cliff. There were so many things we had to keep silent about. That silence bound us together, like an invisible, unbreakable cord making us strong and able to persevere in the face of persecution. I knew I shouldn't answer but I felt so sorry for Brenda now that I knew the truth of her situation.

"Mitch DeLory had a disagreement with the prophet and he was ordered to leave," I said, looking at my fingernails, afraid that the sting and shame of Cliff's departure would show on my face.

"What kind of disagreement?"

"I don't know exactly what it was but my father does, since he's on the council. He told us that Mr. DeLory judged and criticized authority. So his family was reassigned and he left."

"Reassigned? What is that?"

"When a man is expelled from the community, the prophet assigns his wives to a different husband. Mr. DeLory had four wives and a bunch of children who were given to another man."

Brenda looked shocked, shaking her head as if to be sure she heard me correctly. "They were given to another man? Like property, like a car or something?"

"Well, a man's wives *are* his property in a way. They are bound to him for safekeeping and so that he can lead them to heavenly salvation as their priesthood head. When he falls from favor with the prophet, it isn't right that their souls should be lost as well."

"But what about his children? He's their biological father, he has legal rights to see them."

"The prophet says that when a woman and her children are reassigned to a righteous man, God changes their blood and their DNA to match their new father to be sure they gain entrance to the celestial kingdom in the afterlife."

Brenda just stared at me, saying nothing for a long time. Her hand was gripped so tightly on her lemonade glass it looked as if it might break. When she finally spoke, her voice was very soft. "I see. I had no idea."

I wasn't sure where the conversation had gone wrong, but I knew I had been there too long and I still had chores at home, so I stood to excuse myself. The sewing and my questions about BYU would have to wait for another day. "I'll come by soon to help you with your dresses, Brenda."

"That would be nice, Alva. I enjoy your company."

I was beginning to like Brenda, even if she was a little different. It was just because she had been living on the outside. In time, she would be just like the rest of us.

When I got home, I felt Cliff's absence like a heavy stone around my neck. His place at the table was not set. He was not out back with the ax chopping up Pinyon pinewood for the fire. He was not even a topic of conversation or a name mentioned by my siblings or the sister wives. He truly had ceased to exist in our world, and I knew I was not supposed to, but I missed him terribly.

Mama was quiet and subdued as she mashed up the potatoes

while Sister Cora pulled a sausage casserole from the oven. "How is Ann Marie doing?" Sister Cora asked.

I knew better than to mention that I had seen Sister Cora at her brother's house, so I played dumb. "She's much better, Sister Cora."

"Good to hear. My brother deserves a quorum of good wives, not windy-headed girls with a lot of crazy ideas."

"Yes, ma'am."

"You can run out back to the mustard green patch and pick up some for dinner, Alva. Hurry up before it gets any later."

I put on my sweater and went out the back door. The sun had started to go down, casting a magenta hue over the desert. Mustard greens grew wild in a big patch behind our back fence and many families pulled them up to eat, especially near the end of the month when the government-aid checks were running low. As I made my way among the lacy leaves and pale yellow flowers, I saw the familiar sight of Joseph John's checkered shirt approaching, a cloth sack in hand. My heart sped up. He was here and I could tell him the good news about my cycle! I couldn't believe my good fortune and silently thanked God for answering my prayers.

"Hi, Alva Jane!" he said with a surprised smile.

I looked around to see if we were indeed alone. "I have to talk to you. So much has happened," I said.

"I heard about your brother Cliff. My father said he saw him out on the highway. I'm so sorry for you, Alva."

"We dropped him off yesterday morning. It was awful, watching him walk away alone like that. And I've been taking care of Wade Barton's wife because last week we went to the prophet's compound, all the council member families—" I stopped short, unsure if I should talk about Sister Ann Marie's discipline. Joseph John's father was not on the council; his family had not been invited.

"You went to Uncle Kenton's? Inside his house?"

"It was a family matter. But I just want to know, when we're married, if you get sore at me you wouldn't hit me, would you? I mean, not really hard or a lot?"

Joseph John's eyes softened and he reached for my hand, checking over his shoulder to make sure no one was watching. He dropped his voice and said, "I know some of the men here do that, Alva, but not in my family. My father has never raised a hand to any of his three wives and he's taught my brothers and me that we don't need to use our fists to rule our families. There's nothing you could do that would ever make me hit you. All I want to do is make you happy to be my wife and to have a lot of children running around."

I felt a sense of relief wash over me and I fought the impulse to go to Joseph John, to feel his arms slide around me and rest against the safety of his shoulder. "Then you'd best talk to your father right away because I'm no longer a girl. I've become a woman now."

"Your cycle came?"

"Last week. I haven't told anyone except Leigh Ann."

Joseph John looked so happy I thought he would jump three feet in the air. "I'm talking to my father tonight!" he said, turning to go toward home empty-handed.

"Wait! Don't you want any mustard greens?"

We both laughed until we heard Sister Cora's voice calling me from the back porch. "Alva Jane! What are you up to out there?"

Joseph John ducked and moved away from me. We couldn't risk having Sister Cora find us alone. I hurried back toward home, hoping that she hadn't seen us but relieved to know that now Joseph John could talk to his father. It would just be a matter of time until we were married.

CHAPTER EIGHT

THE DAYS FOLLOWING CLIFF'S DEPARTURE SEEMED to drag on interminably. It was not just his absence but my own anxiety and impatience, waiting to hear some word from Joseph John. Five days had passed. I endured the daily trip to Wade Barton's house. Sister Ann Marie's wounds were healing and she had become docile. She sat silent during our sessions, listening as I read from scripture, no longer struggling to speak. Sister Irene approved of this version of Sister Ann Marie, commenting that the Lord was surely working his healing on her spirit. I prayed that this was true, but I couldn't help but see her as depressed and broken.

It seemed that both Sister Irene and Wade Barton were paying me extra attention when I was there. I liked it better when Brother Wade was out of the house and Sister Irene would take

me to the quiet basement room and leave me alone with Sister
Ann Marie. But lately, Brother Wade was often home and he
seemed to be finding reasons to talk to me, asking me about
my work at the store with Mr. Battle or inquiring after Sister
Cora and Sister Emily. Sister Irene asked me about sewing patterns and even offered a new recipe for cooking a corned beef
casserole. I made conversation with them but I tried to keep to
myself as much as I could.

Once I was married to Joseph John and running my own
home as a first wife, I would not have time to do Sister Cora's
bidding. I would have my own family to take care of. But it
had been almost a week and there had been no word from him.
Maybe his father hadn't agreed to our marriage? Maybe Joseph
John had reconsidered, thinking of all the new faces and people
he would be meeting at college? I felt trapped, unable to move
forward with anything. I had never wanted something for myself
as much as I wanted to marry Joseph John. I had always been
happy at home with Mama and the rest of the family, but lately,
things had been changing.

Since the disgrace of Cliff's expulsion, Daddy had not visited
Mama's room, even on her designated night. He complained of
being tired and overworked but I knew that his absence from
my mother's bed was a sign of his displeasure that Cliff had
embarrassed the family in the eyes of the community and the
prophet. Mama did her best to keep sweet, baking special breads
that Daddy favored, wearing the emerald green dress that set off
her hair so beautifully. But still he stayed away and Mama suffered while Sister Cora gloated about it in a million subtle ways.

I prayed every night that life at home would return to normal but it didn't at all. It got worse. June drew to a close and
on the first of July, the government checks arrived. Sister Cora
always made all the sister wives gather around her as she handed
them out, just to rub it in that she was a first wife who didn't
rely on government aid.

With the whole family assembled, Daddy suddenly stepped
into the doorway beside me, giving my hair a toss. "How's my
Gumdrop doing?" he whispered.

I smiled and squeezed his hand. He stepped into the center
of the circle of his wives, cleared his throat, and said, "I have
some important news for everyone. I have had a revelation to
take another wife and I have discussed it with the prophet who
has confirmed it. She is Marcie Barton. I expect you will all welcome her and love her as a sister wife. She is helping us all to
reach the fullness of exaltation in the afterlife."

A new sister wife? Although it was a blessing to bring a new
wife into the family it was always an adjustment, too. Room had
to be made, she had to learn the ways of the family and how the
house ran. Plus, the jealousies ran high as Daddy usually spent
more of his limited time with a new wife.

Marcie Barton was fifteen years old and although my father
had taken young wives before, this was the first time he would
marry a girl I had grown up with. Marcie had sat behind me at
the Zion Academy until she'd dropped out of school last year
to prepare for marriage. She was taller than average and had a
bigger-than-average bosom to match. And Marcie was known
to be something of a flirt. She had felt Sister Emily's ruler on

her knuckles more than a few times for talking with boys in the schoolyard.

I thought back to the night of Sister Ann Marie's discipline and remembered how Daddy's eyes had lingered over Marcie. And how Marcie had met his stare with an open, confident gaze of her own and a little smile. Although I knew it was evil to think on, I couldn't help but wonder what it would be like to have relations with a man my father's age. The very idea repulsed me.

I looked over to see Mama's reaction, knowing this could not have come at a worse time for her. She was always plagued with jealousy when a new wife joined the family, afraid of losing her position as the favorite. With Daddy staying away from her bed already, this time it would be even worse. Mama's smile looked frozen and stiff on her face.

I glanced around the circle of sister wives. Only Sister Cora beamed with satisfaction. Clearly she had been consulted about this marriage beforehand. Marcie was, after all, her niece.

Daddy went on to tell us that the sealing ceremony was to take place within a week. It was settled. As Daddy prepared to leave for the day's work, I saw my mother approach him. I knew she wanted a private word with him but Daddy rebuffed her, brushing her hand from his arm as if she were a bothersome gnat. I felt a flash of pity and sadness. Mama stood watching his broad back disappear out the front door, then turned to me with a smile. "Alva Jane, would you help me bring down the new embroidered linen from the bedroom? I finished it last night and I'd like to use it for tonight's dinner."

I followed her upstairs and once we were in the privacy of our bedroom, Mama's happy exterior vanished.

"Marcie Barton? She's just a bundle of evil impulses waiting to be set free! Have you seen the way she looks at men in the community? That girl has no shame. I've heard the talk, that she's been ready for months now!" Mama spat the words out. I tried to calm her down but she would have none of it.

"And don't think I don't know your father, Alva Jane. I've been married to him for eighteen years and I know the lure of a willing virgin. I was a fourteen-year-old bride myself and your father just can't get enough of that!"

I felt sick to think of my father in such terms and I wanted more than anything for her to be quiet, but it was not my place to say such a thing to her.

"And she is helping us to reach the fullness of exaltation in the afterlife? She's going to help us enter the celestial kingdom?" Mama laughed bitterly. But a moment later, her eyes began to tear. Her voice dropped to a whisper as she caught her reflection in the mirror.

"I've had twelve children in eighteen years, more than any other sister wife in this family. I should be the one honored for helping us to reach the fullness of exaltation, not some young girl with a fire in her privates!"

With these last words Mama threw herself on the bed, and muffled her sobs in a pillow. I sat beside her, smoothing her hair, trying to comfort her. I had never seen her so undone.

How could my mother, the shining example of The Principle at work, be reduced to this?

My mother had always seemed to me so confident, so powerful among the sister wives. How could such a woman be brought so low by the arrival of a teenage girl? After eighteen years of marriage, was there really nothing more to Mama than being a jewel in Daddy's heavenly crown that lost its luster on a husband's whim or ill temper? The Principle of plural marriage is supposed to be the highest form of fulfillment and satisfaction that a woman can attain; once she is safely ensconced in its protective fold, she will be a queen for all eternity. How many times had my father told me, *"Never give up your quest for queendom, Alva Jane."*

I looked at my mother sprawled across the faded bedspread. I saw someone altogether different from who I had seen before. She looked nothing like a queen; she looked like a woman who had birthed twelve children and rose before dawn each day to begin her work, a woman tired and frightened and helpless.

"Don't worry, Mama. It will be just like it was with Sister Mona and Sister Eulalia. Marcie won't keep Daddy's interest for long."

Mama lay there prone for a long time without a word. Then she sat up, wiping her eyes, adjusting her dress. When she finally spoke, her voice was hard and dry, a caustic whisper. "Not if I have anything to do with it she won't. That girl may be hot to go, but I know your father like the back of my hand. I know what pleases him, what doesn't. We must all do our best to regain your father's favor. He chose Marcie Barton because she is the prophet's niece. He wants to ingratiate himself to Uncle Kenton, to cement the ties with his family. You must keep extra sweet, Alva Jane. Agree with everything that Sister Cora or any of the others ask of you. Once the tide has shifted back in our favor, you'll get your reward. I promise you."

Then Mama climbed onto a stepladder, reached into the top shelf of the armoire, and took down a beautifully embroidered tablecloth. "Let's take our handiwork downstairs, shall we?" she said with a big smile, and had I not seen her distress a few moments before, I would not have believed she had shed even one tear.

As we walked downstairs, Mama's words about why Daddy chose Marcie stuck like a sharp stick in my mind. I had never considered that my father did anything without the purest of motives, to serve God. Now my own mother had said differently. I wished she had never said those words and even less that I had listened to them.

The rest of the day the house was filled with the sister wives' chattering and speculation about Marcie Barton. My mother kept silent. I was relieved when Sister Cora asked me to run an errand to the Pineridge store to pick up some tar soap for Sister Emily's eczema. I would pass Brenda Norton's house on the way, and if I hurried, I would have time to drop by and ask her about BYU while helping her set up her sewing machine.

When I arrived, she looked even more unhappy than she had the last time I was there. She invited me in but I could see she was all out of sorts. When I took her sewing machine out and started to thread the bobbin, she wanted to take notes, but she was so distracted that she kept looking for a pencil and didn't realize she had one tucked behind her ear! I got the bobbin in and the foot in place, then I started on some simple straight stitches so she could see how to make them, but when she tried the threads got all tangled up and then she stood up suddenly, pushing the fabric away.

"I can't do this, it's useless!" she cried.

"Don't worry. It's not easy at first but you'll get the hang of it," I reassured her.

"It's not just this sewing, it's everything, Alva. Jack came home yesterday and said that the prophet has decided it's time for him to take a second wife!" From the look on her face, Brenda didn't think this was good news, even if it meant that she would be exalted. I remembered what Sister Cora had said, that people who have lived outside plural marriage struggle with it. Even my mother, who comes from four generations of polygamy, was all upset over Marcie Barton joining the family.

"That's good, Brenda. He needs only one more to get into the celestial kingdom in the afterlife."

"One more?" She looked horrified.

"Three wives is the minimum required for a godly man to be exalted and lead you to salvation as well."

Brenda began to pace and wring her hands. When she spoke it was as if she was talking to herself as much as she was talking to me. "I asked him to wait. He told me before we came here that we'd have a long time to settle in before we moved into plural marriage, that I'd be able to adjust. But now he says that the prophet has decided and we must accept his revelation. And that if I can't make this adjustment with a whole and happy heart, that I can go back to my parents in Salt Lake as a divorced woman!"

With that she sat on the edge of the sofa and burst into tears. It was the second time in one day I had seen a woman crying over The Principle. I could imagine how hard it must be for her, how alone she must have felt in Pineridge with no friends, unable to do the things that all women do. Brenda's hand shook as she reached out for mine.

"How do they do it, Alva? Your mother and the other sister wives? I know it is normal for all of you who have been born into it, but the idea of having another wife living under our roof is so hard for me."

I thought of Mama, lying across the bed at home, crying over Marcie Barton. "It's not all sponge cake and sweet cream," I said, and that made her smile. "My mother is struggling mightily with the idea of a new sister wife joining our family next week."

"Your father is taking another wife?"

"Marcie Barton. She's my age."

Brenda's eyes widened in surprise. "And how old is that?"

"Fifteen. I'm still fourteen but I'll be fifteen in a few months."

"What about the age of consent?"

I had no idea what she was talking about. "Whatever that is, we don't have it here."

"Of course you do, Alva. The age of consent is the legal age at which a person can marry. It's eighteen in most states and it's the law, even here in Utah."

"But how can the law decide when you can or can't marry?" I asked.

"It's designed to protect young people, especially girls, from being pushed or forced into marriage before they are mature enough to make up their own minds."

I'd never heard of such a thing and I knew Brenda must be wrong. I had known so many girls my age and even younger who had married. There was no way we had that law in Pineridge and I said so. But Brenda shook her head.

"It's the law of the state, Alva. Pineridge is in Utah so the law applies here as well."

Now I knew why we lived by God's law rather than the laws of the state. Imagine if the state said I couldn't marry Joseph John until I was eighteen? He'd be long gone at college by then with a Gentile wife and a whole flock of children.

"Law or no law, she's being sealed to my father next Wednesday. And my mama was crying over it just like you are. But it will pass and then you'll get used to it. Everyone does."

"But how?" she asked.

"Because we have to" was the only answer I could think of.

Plural marriage wasn't a choice, it was a scriptural requirement. We all did it, as I would with Joseph John.

Brenda sighed. "You know, Alva, this is my fault. If I had been able to have children, Jack never would have fallen in with the fundamentalists back home. He started going to their meetings because he was so upset that we couldn't have a family. And that's when the idea of plural marriage took hold in his mind. And you know what my parents did when they found out that we were moving here, that Jack had signed over our condominium and bank accounts to the Brotherhood? My good, faithful Mormon parents?"

I shook my head.

"They gave me the name of a divorce lawyer! But I married until death do us part, Alva. And I have to make this work even if I can't see how to do it right now."

I patted her hand. "Don't worry, Brenda, you'll find your way. And who knows? Maybe God will reward your faithfulness with a baby of your own!"

Her eyes got all teary again. "You'll come by to visit me from time to time, won't you, Alva? I do enjoy your company. Now tell me something good, something happy about you. Do you have a sweetheart? A boy you have a special feeling for?"

It was as if Brenda had reached right into my mind and pulled out my very thoughts at that moment. She had that way about her, of asking questions and saying things that made me think about my own feelings, my own life. I hadn't told anyone about Joseph John and our plans to marry, but now the words just spilled out of me, like the bag of alphabet letters that Mama puts into the vegetable soup.

"His name is Joseph John Hilliard and he's talking to his father this week to get permission to go to the prophet. We hope to marry before he goes to BYU in the fall. There are so many questions that I have to ask you about Provo and the university. . . ."

Before I could get any further, we heard the front door open. Jack Norton stepped into the house, and when he saw me, his

107

face lit up in a big crocodile smile. "Alva Jane, how nice of you to come by!"

I stood to go. I didn't want to be around Jack Norton, especially now that the prophet had decided it was time for him to take another wife. The last thing I wanted was for him to set his sights on me. "I was just leaving, Mr. Norton. Brenda is making good progress with her sewing."

Brenda winked at me and Jack smiled even more. "That's terrific! I hope you can come by regularly to help her. I knew it would just be a matter of time before she fit in."

I thought of how he had told Brenda she could go back home divorced if she didn't go along with plural marriage. And I knew suddenly that he didn't really love her. If he did, he would have been gentler with her, coming from the outside and all. He would have helped her understand that she needed plural marriage for her own salvation rather than threatening her with a shameful divorce in the eyes of God and man. I tried to imagine Joseph John treating me that way and I couldn't, for which I was thankful.

I headed out the door, feeling more confused than ever. I knew that we were God's chosen people and that keeping the covenant of plural marriage was the foundation of our lives, but after seeing my mother and Brenda so upset, I was beginning to see that The Principle may light the way to salvation, but it casts a long shadow as well. Until now, I had known that there were tensions within the family over Daddy's affections, but I had never seen the kind of despair that Brenda and my mother were suffering. Maybe it was always there and I had been too young to notice it. But now that my own marriage was close at hand, it worried me.

I arrived at the Pineridge store for the tar soap just as Joseph John came around the corner onto Main Street, returning from public school. He had his backpack slung over one shoulder, his nose buried in a book, and he looked like he'd grown another inch in the last week. He looked up to see me heading into the store and followed me in. The store was half-full and we moved carefully down the rows of merchandise, maneuvering for a meeting spot where no one would pay much attention.

With the soap in hand, I stopped in front of the hair elastics, looking for a little something to take to Ann Marie Barton. Joseph John wandered over. He stopped beside me and whispered, "Alva Jane, meet me behind the barn before dark. I have something to tell you."

I searched his face for some sign of what the news might be and I could see by the way his eyes smiled at me, it was good. Good news! Which meant he had spoken to his father and Mr. Hilliard had agreed to our marriage. I knew that once we had the prophet's approval, everything would get better. I would no longer be just a daughter caught in the troubles and tensions among my parents and the other sister wives. I would be a first wife, making my own home, my own family.

I touched my hand against his as a sign of consent and then turned to run smack-dab into Wendy Callers, who had come sneaking up behind us, pretending to look for a hairbrush. Had she overheard Joseph John? Had she seen my hand on his? If so, she gave no sign. She nodded politely and said, "Good day, Alva," and moved on. I didn't give her a second thought. All I had room for in my heart and my mind was the knowledge that I was just a few steps away from beginning my real life, doing my duty before God and to my husband.

CHAPTER NINE

THE SUN WAS BEGINNING TO SINK LIKE A YELLOW ball of fire in the sky. Through the open window of the kitchen I felt the chill that crept over the desert as evening approached. I opened a can of my mother's sweet onions and emptied them into the pot on the stove. My sisters were setting the table and bringing in the clean wash from the line. I needed to find a way to get out of the house to meet Joseph John at the barn.

"Mama, I'm thinking some mustard greens would be good with dinner tonight," I suggested.

"We have canned onions and peas, that's enough."

"I think something fresh would be good, that's all," I pushed.

"Well, if you really want them, go on and get them. I don't know where the others are. If they don't come back soon I'll have to call those girls out back and have them eat here in the main house so as not to waste anything."

Mama was annoyed. Sister Cora and Sister Emily must have gone to visit Rita Mae and the new baby. They were always back well before sundown to begin the evening meal, but today they must have lingered.

"I'll be right back, Mama," I said, running out the door.

I raced toward the livestock barn where the community's horses and cows were kept. It was just a ways outside of the center of town. Sundown was rapidly approaching, the sky shifting color to the purplish hue of twilight that made the desert look as if the hand of God Himself had painted it. The red rocks surrounding Pineridge were slowly turning into shadows. I looked over my shoulder as I drew near to the barn, making sure there was no one to see me.

I knew it was wrong to meet Joseph John alone like this, but I was so close to seeing my dream fulfilled, I just had to find out what his news was. I slipped around the side of the barn and there he was, pacing in front of the boxed doors that led into the interior. His face lit up when he saw me.

"I'm so glad you came, Alva. I have been wanting to get word to you all week. My father agreed that my dream was a revelation from God, and he's going to speak to your father and the prophet this evening about us getting married!"

These were the words I had been waiting to hear for as long as I could remember! After years of thinking on it, dreaming of it, the time had finally come. We were going to be married! In my excitement I leaned forward into Joseph John's arms. As my lips brushed against his, I suddenly felt a strong hand grip my collar, yanking me backward. I lost my footing and flailed, regaining it just in time to come face to face with the blazing blue eyes of Sister Cora.

My heart froze; I couldn't find any words to say. How did she know I was here? Wendy Callers must have heard and told her, there was no other explanation. Now I knew why Sister Cora wasn't at home helping Mama in the kitchen. She had been waiting to catch me here with Joseph John. Sister Emily stood behind her, her skinny arms crossed over her chest.

"A deceitful and wayward girl brings the greatest shame to her family's name, in the eyes of the Lord and the prophet," Sister Cora said, twisting my arm behind my back and giving me a firm shove toward home.

"It's not like you think, Sister Cora," I tried to explain, but she silenced me with a stinging slap to my face.

"You do not talk until you've been given permission."

Sister Cora kept a tight grip on me and Sister Emily followed behind Joseph John, who walked with his head hung low. Neither of us was allowed to explain what we were doing behind the barn alone, in violation of all the rules. My cheek still felt the sting where Sister Cora had slapped me and I heard her whispering as we walked, calling me a slew of filthy names and insults. My eyes burned with tears of shame but I dared not cry out loud.

Why had I been so stupid and reckless to agree to meet Joseph John alone? Why hadn't I waited for a better, safer moment? I had no idea what would happen now. I could only pray that my parents would understand. They had known Joseph John all his life and they knew that I was a good, obedient girl. Once we got home, we would contact Mr. Hilliard and the whole thing would be worked out. It had to be worked out.

We walked in the door to find Daddy seated at the kitchen table with Mama, Sister Susannah, and the children. They looked up in shock to see us in such a state: Sister Cora gripping my arm, Joseph John with his eyes downcast in guilt. I saw their minds race to the worst possible conclusion. The look on Mama's face chilled me to the core; she believed the worst.

"Oh, Mama, it's not what you think at all—," I began, my voice trembling with tears.

Sister Cora cut me off. "I caught these two behind the livestock barn, Eldon Ray. Alva Jane was kissing this boy, kissing him full on the lips! They made a secret plan to meet earlier today and luckily I heard about it in time to prevent any further damage to our family name by this stupid child!"

Daddy's face lost all its color and he gripped the sides of the kitchen table, his knuckles white.

"If I may, Mr. Merrill, I want to explain," Joseph John spoke up, his tone respectful, cautious. "I have no ill intentions with Alva Jane, I had a dream, a revelation that we are to be married and I spoke to my father about it this week. He is coming to speak to you this evening."

He got no further before my father rose, his full stature filling the room. "You had a revelation, young man? And based on that, you thought that you could choose who to marry, that you made that decision? Are you the prophet? Are you the divine revelator in this community? If we can all count on your revelations, what do we need Kenton Barton for?"

"I meant no disrespect to the prophet, Mr. Merrill, it's just that Alva and I have known each other all our lives. She's done nothing to be ashamed of."

Despite my fear, I felt such a rush of pride in Joseph John, speaking up for me and in the face of my powerful father, no less!

"And I'm to take your word for that, I suppose? I'm supposed to believe that you with your masculine needs and desires were content just to be near my virtuous daughter?" Daddy's cruel, mocking tone cut straight into my heart. He thought ill of me and I could not bear it.

"Daddy, I've done nothing—," I began, but my father silenced me with a cold stare.

"Is Sister Cora lying then, Alva Jane? You weren't out at the livestock barn with this boy? She didn't see you kiss him on the mouth?"

I couldn't deny those things had happened, but not the way Daddy made them sound. "No, sir. Sister Cora isn't lying, it's just not the way it seems. . . ."

My father stopped me, holding up a hand. "You've admitted your guilt, Alva, and there is nothing more for you to say. You're to be punished, you're to feel the pain of the rod so you do not bring shame to this family again!"

Sister Emily moved to the phone. "I'm calling the boy's father, to have him come and pick him up."

But Daddy took the phone from her. "Not yet, Emily. Aaron

Hilliard knew perfectly well that his son had these designs on my daughter and he did not come to me first. I'll handle this boy."

I saw Joseph John brace himself for a beating but Daddy just grabbed him by the scruff of his shirt and dialed the phone. Given his size and strength, he held Joseph John immobile with no effort at all.

"Tom?" he said when someone picked up the other end of the line. "This is Eldon Ray. I've had some trouble with one of these boys and my daughter, Alva Jane. . . . Aaron Hilliard's boy, Joseph John . . . I'm taking them out to the livestock barn. Meet me there with anyone else you can round up."

He hung up the phone and motioned for my mother. "Take her out to the car and wait with her."

Mama grabbed my wrist and moved me to the door while Daddy shoved Joseph John ahead of him. Outside night had fallen and the four of us walked silently out to the Impala.

I sat still beside my mother in the backseat as my father began the drive back to the livestock barn. I was afraid to move, afraid to speak. My plans had all gone so horribly wrong. I had never seen my parents this way. Like any child I had been spanked for wrongdoing, like when I was six and I opened three cans of Sister Cora's peaches and ate only half of them. But it had been years since I had been punished with a serious whipping and I dreaded not only the pain but also the humiliation, especially in front of Joseph John. To be whipped like a five-year-old before the boy I hoped to marry was too awful to imagine.

I wept in fear and frustration as I looked out the window at the desert now blanketed in darkness. The flowering yucca that lined the road stood like women in white, witnesses to my trial. Daddy pulled the Impala up to the livestock barn and I saw the bright headlights of a truck, waiting. My father stepped out first and went to meet the men who had gathered, answering his call. In the bizarre shadows thrown by the lights of the truck I made out the faces of Tom Pruitt, Leon Jayne, Eddie Raynard. They were men on the council, men my father's age. Hulking behind them I saw Wade Barton and my knees went weak.

Why had Daddy called them out here? Did he intend to have an audience to watch my whipping? My father came back to the car and pulled Joseph John out by his arm, pushing him toward the group of men.

"Take him out beyond the red rock ridge and teach him a lesson," Daddy said, and then I knew why the men had come. I felt a sick drop in my stomach as panic swept over me.

Beyond the red rock ridge there was a natural sand pit, a big hollow that swallowed up all sound and light. It was no-man's-land, a place where any cries for help would echo off the rocks and evaporate, unanswered. The six men Daddy had called were going to whip Joseph John for his trespass, to do who knew what harm to him.

"Daddy, please don't. He didn't do anything, I swear—"

My mother pinched hard at the soft flesh of my underarm to silence me and I cried out in pain.

Tom Pruitt and Leon Payne pinned Joseph John's arms and forced him into the cab of the pickup truck. The other men jumped into the open truck bed. In the stark light of the

MICHELE DOMINGUEZ GREENE

Impala's high beams, they looked like gargoyles, their faces tight and twisted with anger. My father waited until the truck taillights had disappeared before he motioned for Mama to lead me inside the livestock barn.

The barn was dark and smelled of hay, cow dung, and the rank, gamy scent of the beasts themselves. My father pulled a chain to light a single bulb that hung from the middle of a wooden beam, then led me to a back stall.

"So this is where you planned to meet up with your young man, Alva Jane? Out here in the filth, where these beasts of burden live and sweat? And what were you two planning to do out here, all alone?" He began removing his belt from his pants.

"Daddy, we weren't planning anything. Joseph John just wanted to tell me that he had spoken to his father and—"

"If you weren't doing anything bad, then why were you hiding out here? You were planning to do more than kiss that boy and you know it!"

"No, Daddy! It was just a little kiss, it wasn't anything!"

"If you think kissing boys isn't anything, then you have a thing or two to learn, Alva Jane," my father said, running the water hose over his belt, wetting it down.

I covered my face and burst into tears, terrified. "Please, Daddy. I'm sorry, I'll never do anything like that again."

"Oh, I know you won't, Alva Jane, I'm going to make very sure of that," he said, bringing the belt down hard against the back of my legs. It struck hard and wrapped around my calves, burning like a branding iron. I screamed in pain.

"Daddy, stop! I promise, I pro—"

118

I didn't get another word out before my father brought the strap down again, hitting me behind the knees. I fell forward onto the barn floor, smearing my dress with the filth of the livestock.

He shouted, "How did you think I would allow you to marry an untested boy like Joseph John Hilliard? How is he going to help you to be exalted, a boy who has done nothing to prove his worth to the prophet or the Lord?"

The belt strap hit again, this time across my back. I cried out, my mouth filling with the taste of the hay, the dirt, and dung on the floor. "Mama, help me, please!"

My mother grabbed my hands, pulling me to my feet as I tried to curl myself into a protective ball. "You come from five generations of living The Principle, Alva Jane," my mother said through gritted teeth. "*You* do not presume to take a sweetheart, to think that *you* can choose who to marry. The prophet decides your future, *you* do not. And now you have behaved like a whore, meeting a boy in secret, bringing even more disgrace to this family. . . ." Mama dug her nails into my wrist. I pulled back, but her grip was surprisingly strong.

"Please, Mama, I won't—"

Then I heard the belt slicing through the still air inside the barn and it hit, cutting through the fabric of my dress and grazing the flesh of my shoulders. I looked into my mother's eyes, shiny and metallic, and saw a person I did not recognize.

In that moment I knew there would be no mercy, no relief, until my father's rage was spent. That this was the price to pay for having dared to think I could choose whom to marry. It was as Mama said: The prophet chose for me, for everyone. I fell again to my knees and curled into a ball to ward off the remaining blows, which came swiftly now.

Finally, my father grew weary and let his arms drop down to his sides. He was wet with sweat as he pulled his belt through the loops of his pants.

"Take her to the root cellar. Let her spend the night in there alone to think about her future," he said, pushing the barn doors open and heading out into the cold night air without so much as a glance back.

Mama helped me up to my feet and led me to the back of the barn, pulling open the door to the cellar. A steep stairway led to total blackness below. I was afraid to go down; who knew what snake or other animal might be hiding down there? My mother grabbed my arm and guided me down the narrow steps. It took a moment for my eyes to adjust. Against the earthen walls, I saw burlap bags of potatoes and other bins of winter vegetables.

In the darkness, my mother whispered, "I'm so disappointed in you, Alva. I asked for your help in winning back your father's favor and this is how you answer me. You've jeopardized the position of your siblings, all of us, in this family."

I made my way to the corner of the cellar and curled myself against the cold wall. Mama stormed back up the steps, pausing at the top.

"Your father and I only did what we had to tonight, Alva. You've gotten yourself into a dangerous place with that Hilliard boy. I only hope that through your father's influence we are able to save your good name and standing in the community. Be thankful that we care enough to take up the rod to lead you back to safety."

With that, she closed the door, leaving me in total darkness. I heard her footsteps as she retreated, then the engine of the car firing up and disappearing in the distance.

Once I knew they were gone, a wild, ragged wail came from someplace deep inside me that felt as if it had no end. The pain from the belt was terrible but the pain in my heart was worse. Shame, fear, anger, and disbelief all jumbled together. I cried until my voice became a hoarse whimper.

I lay my body against the cellar floor and closed my eyes. I heard the scurrying of rodents as they moved through the stalls above me. I could not escape the image of Joseph John being forced into the truck and driven off by those hateful men. I had suffered so much at just my father's hand. Joseph John would face the fury of six angry men in a dark corner of the desert. Was he alive or dead? Had they left him out there, injured and alone, at the mercy of the coyotes and other predators? I couldn't bear to think of it. I did not care if I lived or died. I just wanted to escape from the pain and the memory of my father's face, his belt swinging overhead, my mother's eyes cold and hard as glass.

CHAPTER TEN

I AWOKE SUDDENLY TO A SHAFT OF LIGHT COMING in as the cellar door was yanked open. I lifted my head from the floor and squinted, my eyes adjusting to see my mother's smiling face.

"Mama's here to take you home, Alva Jane. I hope you had a good long time to think about how to set yourself right with the Lord."

I didn't move, staring at her broad smile. *Why is she smiling?* Maybe everything had been cleared up. Maybe my parents now understood that nothing had happened behind the barn with Joseph John. Maybe he had been given a chance to explain to the men before they beat him up.

"Come on, baby," Mama said, taking my arm and leading me out into the breaking sunrise.

I followed, still dazed and confused by my mother's arrival and tenderness. I allowed Mama to settle me into the Impala where she held my hand and stroked my dirty hair while she drove toward home.

"It's all going to be fine, Alva Jane. Daddy and Mommy have fixed everything, you'll see."

I felt the warm rumbling of the car as we headed for home. This was the Mama I knew and loved and who loved me. *Daddy and Mommy have fixed everything.*

My eyes grew heavy and my head settled against her shoulder as sleep settled over me.

Back at home, Mama drew a warm bath. She removed my torn, bloody dress and settled me into the tub. The water stung my welts something fierce at first, but soon they felt better. Mama worked the lather of the shampoo through my loose hair.

"Last night your Daddy felt so bad about having to give you that whipping, Alva Jane, he really did. All he wants for you is to be exalted and to live The Principle, to be happy and fulfilled in the role that God intended for you."

I leaned against the porcelain tub, luxuriating in the feel of my mother's hands against my scalp, washing away the grime of the night before. Washing away the terror and the hurt and the streaks where my tears had mingled with the muddy floor of the barn.

"And last night we sat and discussed this situation and your father has prayed on it and come up with the perfect way to make it right for everyone. I know he's feeling relieved"—Mama's voice dropped to a whisper—"because late last night he came to my room for the first time in weeks! These past few weeks have been so hard for him with the pressures of the Arizona community and the trouble with your brother. He's a good man, Alva Jane. Now that you'll be getting married, you'll learn that patience is a virtue that no wife can live without. You have to forgive your husband so many things. . . ." She sighed.

I would be getting married soon. Getting married! God had heard me in the dark of the root cellar and had taken mercy upon me. Somehow it had all been worked out and Joseph John and I had been forgiven. No doubt my father felt awful for having treated me so roughly, just like Mama said.

After the bath, my mother applied salve and bandages to my back and legs then helped me into a clean dress. She braided my damp hair into a single thick plait and kissed the top of my head like she used to when I was a little girl.

"Let's go downstairs, Alva Jane. We'll wait for Daddy to come back from speaking with the prophet."

We went down to the kitchen table, where the sister wives and Leigh Ann were seated in a circle doing the mending. I took up a pair of work pants and looked around the table, watching the familiar and comforting rhythmic motions of their hands as they worked the needles through the fabric. Everyone was seated in her usual spot. The smell of clean, fresh clothes hanging outside wafted in the open window. Life was just as it had always been. I heard my father's footstep in the hall and in the next moment he appeared in the doorway with a bouquet of fresh flowers.

"How are Eldon Ray's girls today?" he asked. He took his seat at the head of the table and tapped his fingers excitedly.

"Well, I have some big news for two young ladies today. I just came from speaking with the prophet. Leigh Ann and Alva Jane, you are about to become wives and to serve the prophet as God intended."

Leigh Ann smiled broadly and blurted out, "Who am I to marry, Daddy?

"Now, I don't want you to be concerned that he is new to living The Principle. I spoke to Uncle Kenton about it and he feels confident that he is indeed a righteous man, devout in keeping the covenants. You will become the second wife of Jack Norton."

I gasped. I thought of Brenda's tears, her anxieties about bringing a new sister wife into their home. Leigh Ann squealed with happiness and hugged Sister Cora. At least Jack Norton was attractive and barely thirty years old. Then Daddy looked to me.

"Last night I know we passed through a terrible fire of physical punishment, Alva, and I want you to know that it hurt me more than it hurt you. But God came up with a solution, which He has revealed to us."

Mama reached out and took my hand and I waited to hear the words that would make everything right.

Then Daddy said, "You are to become the sixth wife of the prophet's brother, Wade."

Married to Wade Barton? As a sixth wife?

I felt as if I had been struck. I couldn't speak. My parents' smiling faces became blurred and I felt my heart beating fast, too fast. I had to steady myself from falling clean out of the chair.

"See? She's overcome," Mama said, squeezing my hand. All I could do was shake my head. I found my voice but it came out fluttery and weak.

"Wade Barton? I can't marry Wade Barton, he's . . ."

I couldn't find the words to name all the reasons I couldn't marry him! I was terrified of him. I couldn't bear to be in his presence, let alone be his wife.

I saw my father's good humor evaporate as he stared at me across the table. "What are you saying, Alva Jane? That you can't marry Wade Barton? The prophet has decreed that you will be his next wife."

"But Joseph John had a revelation that we were to be married just like you did about Marcie."

My father stood up. "And you expect me, a council member, to hold that young boy's revelations on par with the prophet's or my own? He had impure intentions, Alva Jane. He would have ruined your chances at reaching the celestial kingdom had I not intervened."

"That's not true, Daddy," I protested, but my father's voice boomed, cutting me off.

"Do not presume to tell me what is true and what is not! You are a young girl unschooled in the ways of the world and your own religion, it seems. You think that you and that boy know what is best for you? Well, you can forget Joseph John Hilliard. He has been expelled from the community. The prophet decreed it today and notified his father. You will never see him again."

My head spun and I feared I might faint. Joseph John expelled? I began to shake, as I looked around the table at the hostile faces of the sister wives and my father and mother staring back at me. Joseph John was gone and I was alone.

"But I can't marry Wade Barton, I just can't," I whispered.

"Of course you can't yet, your cycle hasn't started. I made it clear that I will not go against The Principle and let you be taken as a wife before your bleeding begins," my father said.

I looked to Leigh Ann across the table. She locked eyes with me but said nothing. She was the only one who knew that my cycle had begun, and with every fiber of my body I willed her to stay quiet as our father continued, "Leigh Ann will be sealed to Jack Norton in the temple next week, the same day that I take Marcie Barton as my eighth wife. If your cycle has begun by then, all three sealing ceremonies will be performed the same day."

Mama took my arm. "I'll take Alva Jane up to our room. This news has been a shock to her and she clearly is not herself. She is grateful to have received such a blessing, to be taken into the family of the prophet through her fortuitous marriage."

I resisted but my mother guided me toward the stairway, her nails cutting into the flesh of my arm. As we climbed the stairs I looked back to Leigh Ann, my eyes pleading.

Please don't tell them.

CHAPTER ELEVEN

MAMA HELD HER PALM AGAINST MY BACK, PRESSING into the welts from Daddy's belt. I winced at the pain and also at my mother's words. "I will not have you jeopardizing the well-being of anyone in this family with your willful selfishness!"

We reached the bedroom door and Mama gave me a shove inside, pointing to the bed where I was to sit. Then she locked the door behind us and turned to me. "Do you think you're the only one to develop a crush on some handsome young boy in the community? It happens to all of us, but there comes a time to put aside childish ways, Alva Jane, and this is that time."

"But Mama—"

"You have no idea how lucky you truly are. Your marriage to Wade Barton will exalt you in the eyes of the Lord. It is a duty and a *privilege* to live this way, Alva. Do you think the Brotherhood of the Lord always lived in a prosperous, gated community like this? My parents lived in tents, with no running water, no heat. They suffered persecution and police raids, to live as God intended. You come from five generations of plural marriage, and no daughter of mine will break that covenant with God! You will marry Wade Barton and be glad of it, that you had the chance to be taken in by the brother of the prophet!"

"Mama, I'm scared of him. Please don't make me marry a man like that."

"What has gotten into you? You're just a slip of a girl not even fifteen years old yet."

My mind worked frantically, looking for some argument.

"What about the age of consent? I'm not eighteen, it would be illegal for me to marry him."

Mama's eyes narrowed, they looked like two coals spitting fire.

"Who have you been talking to and getting such ideas from, girl? The age of consent means nothing if your parents agree that you are to be married. Those Gentile lawyers always try to use that, changing laws, trying to catch us in their snares. Your father and I could have married you off at twelve if we had wanted and that's what we should have done!"

I reached out for her hand. "Mama, you have no idea what his home is like, it's like a prison. His eyes look crazy and you didn't see up close what he did to Sister Ann Marie. . . ."

She pushed my hand away. "What happened to Ann Marie she did to herself by trying to leave the bonds of a sacred marriage. Wade Barton is not to blame for reining in the wayward spirit of his wife, *she* is!"

"But Mama, I can't imagine being a wife to him, he's repulsive!"

My mother settled her hands on her hips and laughed. "And who are you to judge what makes a man, Alva Jane? Because Joseph John Hilliard won your heart with his boyish charm and his pretty ways? It's a good thing he was expelled. He was getting to be too big for his britches, thinking he could win the affections of all the young girls. You are not the only one who set her eyes on him, my girl."

Her words were meant to hurt me and they did. Still, I whispered back, "But I am the only one he loved."

Then Mama crouched down in front of me, her eyes filled with more fear than anger. When she spoke, her voice had lost its hard edge. "Do you have any idea what it is to be a wife who is not the favorite? To live like Sisters Eulalia or Susannah or even worse, Sister Sherrie? Do you think all of your father's children enjoy the same privileges as we do, living in the big house, with enough food to eat at each meal? Do you ever wonder why we only eat with the entire family on Sundays? Because there is not enough to go around, Alva Jane. Your father gives the lion's share of his time, his money, and his love to us, even though I am a fourth wife. For the sake of your siblings and me, you must marry Wade Barton and please your father. As my daughter you are a reflection of me and after the trouble with your brother, we cannot afford to upset your daddy anymore."

"But Daddy loves you, Mama. There's nothing I can do that would change that. You'll always be the favorite," I said.

Mama laughed again. "With a new fifteen-year-old wife

joining the family next week? You think it will be easy for me to maintain my place in his affections or to hold his interest? You have a lot to learn about life and about men, Alva Jane. Trust your mother. You will come to love Wade Barton and to see his good qualities. You must keep sweet and agree with a cheerful heart to marry him. You must please him and do what you can to win and keep his favor. Now go on downstairs and tell your daddy what he wants to hear."

I sat stock-still, unable to move. I thought of my sisters Carlene and Liza, Laura Jean and Olive, my brothers and the babies. I didn't want any of them to suffer on my account. But as much as I loved them, I could not bring myself to do what Mama asked. The words stuck in my throat like melted wax but I forced them out. "I can't do it, Mama."

My mother stood. When she spoke, her voice was deadly calm. "It is not a question of what you will or will not do, Alva. It has been decided. You will marry Wade Barton if I have to drag you to the temple and stand you up before the prophet myself. It is not your choice, understand that. It is God's will for you. Reconcile yourself to it. You're not to come down to the dinner table this evening."

With that she turned and left the room.

My stomach growled. I hadn't eaten anything since the previous day—since before the kiss, before the beating, before my life crumbled apart. I cracked open the door and tried to catch a whiff of the food downstairs. It smelled like pot roast, Sister Cora's specialty when Daddy brought money home. I knew my

mother had forbidden me to come to dinner in hopes of breaking my will, but it would take more than an empty stomach to
make me marry Wade Barton. Just the thought of it took away
my appetite.

Up in our room alone, I had time to think. And the more
I thought, the more I realized that this nightmare was Sister
Cora's work. I thought back to the day I overheard her praising
me to Sister Irene, Wade Barton's first wife. I'd stupidly believed
she'd had a change of heart toward me. Instead, she was laying
the groundwork for my marriage to her brother. Surely, Wendy
Callers's gossip had not been idle, it had given Sister Cora a
reason to keep an eye on me, to look for anything she could use
against me and push me into her brother's quorum of wives.
And in meeting Joseph John at the barn, I had given her exactly
what she'd wanted.

I imagined her high forehead and her white skin with those
blue eyes, still and quiet like the surface of a lake, hiding the
depth of evil and meanness that lived beneath in her heart. I
hated her. In the deepest part of my heart I hated her and I
didn't care if God condemned me for it.

I went to the bedroom window, the one that faced the back
part of our yard. I looked out at the three run-down trailers
where Sisters Eulalia, Susannah, and Mona lived with their children. I had never thought much about their lives out there, I
rarely went out to visit with them other than to round up the
children for church or other family gatherings.

But now it was as if I was seeing them for the first time. Card-
board covered up broken windows and someone had stacked

the empty propane tanks in a rusted heap in the yard. The shade canopy outside Sister Mona's trailer was torn and falling down, propped up with two broomsticks tied together with wire. Sister Susannah's trailer was messy; I'd seen that when I went to fetch her twins. Sister Eulalia's was clean and neat, everything in its place, but it was crowded with all three boys inside. Sister Mona and her daughter, Cindy, had the smallest trailer, with just a double bed in the back corner and a countertop with a two-burner hot plate and a toaster oven. That was all I knew of how they lived out there.

My mother's words echoed in my head. *There is not enough to go around, Alva Jane. . . .* I had never looked in their kitchen cupboards, never wondered what they did when the food stamps ran low at the end of the month.

I had enjoyed my father's favor and his bounty as well. In my own comfort, it had never occurred to me that some of my brothers and sisters went hungry, not while Daddy drove a new car bought last year when Uncle Kenton gave him a bonus. But now I remembered the night last winter when I couldn't sleep and I saw Sister Susannah looking in the trash cans behind the main house, well past midnight. She moved so quietly, taking off the lids and rooting around the garbage inside. At the time, I thought she was just crazy, but now I realized she had probably been looking for scraps of food that we had tossed out.

My head was dizzy with all of these thoughts and I felt like I was spinning with them, trying to hang on to something to keep myself grounded. My father was a righteous man who upheld the highest principles and standards in the Brotherhood. He had taken seven wives and vowed to protect, provide, and care for them. He was above reproach. But my mother's voice kept coming back to me. *There is not enough to go around. . . . You think I'll be able to hold his interest with a new fifteen-year-old wife joining the family?*

Mama's fears were real; I could see it in her eyes and feel it in her voice. And if my mother could so easily be pushed aside for a young girl, then what was her place in our family built upon? If she had borne so many children and was still in jeopardy of losing her position and privileges, then what were her years of obedience and keeping the covenants worth?

I lay down on the bed, putting the pillow over my head to block out the smells of dinner downstairs and my own troubling thoughts. I willed myself to go to sleep but my mind would not stop, imagining the hell of being married to Wade Barton, thinking on Joseph John alone out in the desert. I would never see him again. To lose both him and Cliff was too much to bear. I pushed my face hard into the pillow to muffle the sound of my crying. It could not be true, this could not be my life, married to Wade Barton with Joseph John lost to me forever!

I heard the door creak open. It was Leigh Ann.

"Are you asleep yet, Alva?" she whispered.

"No, not yet. How was dinner?"

"Not so good," Leigh Ann lied to make me feel better about missing it. She came in and sat on the edge of the bed.

"I'm supposed to be getting some yarn from my mom's sewing room, but Sister Emily is reading from the Pearl of Great

Price again so they won't notice if I take an extra minute." She laid her hand on my shoulder.

"I'm so sorry, Alva Jane. I can't believe that Daddy and Sister Maureen are making you marry Wade Barton."

"I'm not going to marry him, no matter what they say."

"How can you go against them? Daddy is our priesthood head. His word is law. And the prophet confirmed it!"

"I don't know how, but I'm not going to do it." I didn't even know what I was saying, I just knew that I could not, would not, go along with marrying a monster. "You won't tell about my cycle, will you? Please don't tell them!" I begged.

"I won't say anything, I promise. But now that they're watching for it, you'll have to come up with something before next month."

She was right. I had to find a way out of this marriage before my next cycle began.

Leigh Ann took my hand and drew close to me. "Alva, you know that Brenda Norton and her husband, Jack. What does he seem like? I've only seen him coming and going from the temple. Is he nice? Is she?"

"She's real nice, just new to the ways of the community. You'll have to teach her to sew, I know that much. And he seems like a good man, according to what everyone says. At least he's good looking!" I didn't mention Jack's crocodile smile or Brenda's anxieties about plural marriage.

Leigh Ann giggled, covering her mouth. "I've got to go. I stole a biscuit for you," she said, drawing a bun from the pocket of her dress. "Don't worry, I'll keep quiet about your cycle."

She put out her pinkie finger and I hooked mine through it. We had been doing that since we were little girls, but I didn't feel like a little girl any longer.

Leigh Ann slipped out the door to join the family downstairs and I could hear the voices of my mother and siblings talking and laughing. For the first time, I was excluded from the family circle. I was on the outside, forbidden to step into the warmth and comfort. I went back to the window to look out at the trailers again. In Sister Mona's window, one dim lamp was lit.

She was out there alone with two-year-old Cindy. What was it like for them with no one else to talk to, to visit with? I stood for a long time, watching and wondering.

CHAPTER TWELVE

THE NEXT WEEK WAS A MISERY. MAMA DID NOT MISS a chance to lecture me about my responsibilities to the prophet and to God, listing all the reasons I had to marry Wade Barton. And when I did not give in, she forbade my siblings to speak to me. I did my chores in silence, without any camaraderie or conversation. I did my best to apply salve to the welts on my back but it was near impossible to do by myself. I climbed into bed at night with no word of affection from the sisters who shared my room.

I learned that sometimes you feel more lonesome when you're surrounded by people than when you're all alone. I knew there was one thing that would restore me to their affections. But I could not do it; I could not agree to marry Wade Barton willingly. I hated being at odds with my mother, who had always been so loving to me. I hated the battle of wills that made the gulf between us bigger each day, but I knew that it was my life that hung in the balance.

If the days were long, the nights were worse. I dreamed of Joseph John, of walking together, of the final fateful meeting behind the barn. Every time, I awoke thinking that the dream was real and a great rush of relief poured over me until I realized that it was not. Everything I had hoped for was gone. The best I could fight for was to save myself from a hellish marriage.

I told myself that my parents would not force me to marry, that they would not be so cruel as to sacrifice me to appease the prophet. But in my heart I knew they would.

My father went to Arizona to help with the new community and planned to return the night before his marriage to Marcie Barton. Sister Cora began sewing Leigh Ann's wedding dress, and Mama, not willing to be outdone, took me to the Pineridge store to buy white dotted swiss for mine. There would be no escaping my fate.

Walking down the streets of my town, I no longer felt at home. In the harsh desert sun, everything looked like a picture, two-dimensional, not real: the smiling faces of the women I passed, the goods in the window at Desert Pipe and Plumbing. Inside, I felt deadness, different and apart from everything and everyone. It was as if I were being swallowed up whole and each day I lost a little bit more of the will to struggle against it. But I had to struggle. I could not go along blindly like Leigh Ann, giggling as she modeled her wedding dress, finishing up a new quilt she would present to Jack Norton after they were sealed as man and wife. I had to find a way out of my marriage. I prayed for a miracle.

At home Mama worked feverishly on my wedding dress, forcing me to stand for the fitting, enlisting my sisters Olive and Carlene to boost my spirits.

"It sure is a lovely dress, Alva. You're going to be the prettiest bride in Pineridge!" Olive crowed, too young to understand what marriage to Wade Barton would mean.

I looked at myself in the mirror and burst into tears. My mother pinched my thigh, hard. "You pull yourself together, Alva Jane. This is no way for a girl to be acting, chosen for marriage by the prophet's brother no less! I'm going to have this dress ready and waiting, hanging in my closet for the day your cycle starts and you become a wife."

My stomach did a somersault, wondering if Mama had any suspicion that my cycle had already come. But with a mouth full of straight pins, her hands working diligently, it seemed she did not know my secret. Time was running out. I had to do something soon.

A few days later, I sat in the temple sealing room, with its pale ivory carpet and big windows of cut glass. The light could come in but what went on inside remained secret, obscured to the outside world. My father and Marcie would take their vows first; Jack and Leigh Ann would follow. If they knew that my cycle had arrived, I would be standing there too, about to become Wade Barton's wife.

The silk-covered chairs were lined up in rows facing the center altar where the bride and groom would take their vows. On either wall, huge gilt-framed mirrors hung. Jack and Leigh Ann, and Daddy and Marcie would see each other's reflections multiplied endlessly, representing eternity. Above us loomed an enormous crystal chandelier. The beauty of the room was awesome; surely we were close to God in such a place. I prayed extra hard for mercy and deliverance from my marriage. And I avoided looking at Brother Wade, who stood with Sister Irene and Marcie as she prepared to take her vows as Daddy's eighth wife.

Seated behind them were Wade Barton's other four wives: Sisters LeNan, Carol, Betsy, and Ann Marie. Sister Ann Marie's hand was still in a splint. The bruises on her face had faded to a putrid yellow. She sat stiffly and when she looked briefly at me across the room, her face stayed blank.

Our family's sister wives filled the first two rows of seats on the other side of the altar. Daddy stood tall across from Marcie Barton in a white dress with a broad, square lace collar. There was something about her that made me feel unsettled, despite her prim dress and hair. Perhaps it was the intensity of her fixed devotion as she gazed up at Daddy. It was as if you could feel her breath, the way her breasts strained against the fabric of her dress. Maybe my mama was right and Marcie Barton had been hot to go for months.

Uncle Kenton began, "Do you, Brother Eldon Ray Merrill, take Sister Marcie Laurel Barton to be your lawful and wedded wife . . . ?"

When Daddy and Marcie laid their hands atop one another, his seven sister wives rose and stood around them, each adding her own hand to show support. I stole a quick glance at the altar and found Wade Barton staring hard at me. He smiled ever so slightly and I looked away, sickened by his attention.

I will not marry him, no matter what my parents and the prophet say.

But in the next moment, I felt lost. To disobey the prophet meant damnation, it meant I had failed God and would never make it to the heavenly kingdom. Who was I if not a good daughter of the FLDS, if I did not live The Principle as God intended? The enormity of my disobedience weighed heavily upon my soul, especially in this sacred room where couples were sealed for all time. My parents knew I would feel this way in this sacred place. That is why they included me, why my mother's hard gaze met mine as she stood in support of Daddy and Sister Marcie. I stood stock-still, but inside I was drowning in doubt of my faith, my family, and most importantly, of myself. Uncle Kenton finished the vows and I heard his voice, like a judgment from God, telling me what I, what all women, were to do:

"Now go forth in light and truth, raising many children in the family order of heaven."

CHAPTER THIRTEEN

AFTER THE SEALING CEREMONIES, THERE WAS A CELE-bration at our home since our household would be gaining Marcie as a wife and losing Leigh Ann as a daughter. As the families moved around the house drinking fruit punch and eating Sister Emily's squash bread, I found Brenda alone on the back porch, staring at the trailers behind the house. "Congratulations, Brenda."

She smiled distractedly at me and pointed to the trailers. "Who lives out there, Alva?"

"Some of my father's wives. See that one with the new awning? It's for Sister Marcie."

There had been quite a bit of wrangling over Sister Marcie's place in the last few days. Sister Cora had been trying to have her move into the main house. Imagine that! An eighth wife living in the main house! Mama put her foot down and Daddy had finally agreed that it would be too crowded. But I could see that Sister Cora was going to keep at it, trying to get Mama pushed into one of the trailers out back.

With my own troubles to think about, I had grown tired of the constant backbiting and competition between them, tired of hearing my mother's complaints about Sister Cora. I knew she was evil made flesh but she wasn't going to change any more than the desert would turn into the sea, so why bother fighting it?

Brenda sat with her long hem falling over her shoes. Someone had loaned her a good-fitting dress for the ceremony and her hair had grown out a bit to make it easier to style in our fashion. At least Leigh Ann could sew well and show her how to make the right clothes. After a long beat of silence Brenda said quietly, "You know Jack has decided that Leigh Ann and I will trade off. One night he'll stay in her room, the next in mine. Her bedroom is right down the hall. I feel like a crazy person already, driving into work in these clothes and stopping outside of town to change into my work suit. I don't know how long I can do it. . . ." Her voice drifted off. I realized that with all the backslapping and congratulations going on inside, she and I were the only two who felt outside all the celebrating. When Jack and Leigh Ann had taken their vows, Brenda looked as if she had eaten a bowl full of glass and it was twisting and cutting her up inside. But she did her duty; she laid her hand atop her husband's and his new bride's. She stepped headlong into The Principle and no one could find fault with her. Only I knew how tormented she was. I felt closer to her now that I was experiencing my own kind of torment.

"I don't know if your husband told you, but Joseph John has been sent away and I'm to marry the prophet's bother, Wade," I whispered.

Brenda reached out for my hand. "I heard that, but I couldn't believe it. Is it really true? Can't you protest?"

"I've been trying, but so far they haven't changed their minds. Now no one in the family talks to me."

Brenda leaned in close to me. "Alva, this isn't right. This isn't religion, it's something else. Remember what I told you? About the age of consent? It's against the law!"

"That's what I told Mama and she got real mad and said that if my parents agree, it's legal."

I heard Sister Emily's voice behind us. "You two ought to come in and join the family; it's no good sitting outside by yourselves," she said, eyeing us suspiciously.

I hated her as much as I hated Sister Cora. I walked past her without a word, wishing every ill upon her and not repenting in my heart. I was losing my faith, my desire to please God, as well as everything else, but I didn't care. Something inside me was changing and I knew it wasn't good, but I felt powerless to stop it.

Late that evening I sat in silence with my mother in our bedroom, a lone lamp lit. It was late, well past my bedtime, but Mama had not given me permission to go to sleep. She was knitting a sweater for Carlene, her fingers working the needles fast and furious as she stole glances out the window to Sister Marcie's trailer, where Daddy had been all evening, celebrating his wedding night.

I remembered her same vigilance at the window when my father married Sister Eulalia and Sister Mona. Earlier today, Mama had kept sweet, helping Sister Marcie to hang her dresses and decorate her trailer, but now she was visibly consumed by jealousy.

I sat clipping photos for a scrapbook I planned to give to Leigh Ann, photos of our childhood, of our many adventures and happy times together. With her gone from the house, I had no confidante, no friend I could trust. I knew time was short; my cycle would soon come again. Sister Cora and Mama were checking my undergarments for any sign of it. I had seen them doing it on wash day. As soon as they knew I was bleeding, they would marry me to Brother Wade within a matter of days. I had no idea who to ask for help. It didn't seem I could count on anyone but myself.

Looking at the photos spread out before me, I wondered if I could live apart, away from my family, my sisters? Without knotting Carlene's long hair into braids each morning? Away from the happy smiles and laughter of the twins when I chased them and tickled their round little bellies? Could I live in a world beyond the rituals and duties that gave my life meaning? Could I live on the outside? I had never imagined something so risky, so dangerous. I had no idea how to navigate life outside of the FLDS. Somewhere, Joseph John was out there, if he was still alive. My brother Cliff was out there.

Maybe I could do it too. Maybe I could join them. Maybe leaving, escaping, was my only chance to break free from the fate that everyone had decided for me, against my will. I would be an apostate, lost to my family, to God forever. Could I endure the pain of it? Make my parents suffer the shame of having a wayward daughter who left the community?

I knew I had to make a decision fast. The faces of my siblings smiled up at me from the pile of photos in my lap as the *click-click* of my mother's knitting needles continued beside me. The house seemed to heave and groan, settling against the dry wind outside. In my heart I knew. It was the only home I had ever known, but I would leave it. I would escape Pineridge in order to save myself, come what may.

In the days that followed, I worked extra hard in the kitchen and around the house. I volunteered to visit Rita Mae, to do whatever errands Sister Cora needed done. I worked and I waited, looking for a chance to escape. But no opportunity presented itself.

How would it? I had no reason to go outside the community. I didn't attend public school or have a job like Brenda. I had no way of getting beyond the compound walls and even if I did, how long until the Pineridge police found me, walking alone along the highway?

At home, the tensions in the house ran high, but at least Mama found something else to be upset about. As she had feared, Daddy had been out in Sister Marcie's trailer every night, neglecting his conjugal duties to his other wives, leaving Mama in a vile humor, impatient and short-tempered. She stopped talking about my duty to God and my marriage to Brother Wade. All she could think of was Daddy and Sister Marcie and what they were doing out there every night.

My chance came the next week. Everyone in the community was preparing for the Pioneer Day celebration. In the FLDS we don't observe Christmas or Easter. The biggest celebration is Pioneer Day. It marks the day in 1847 when Brigham Young first looked out from the mouth of Emigration Canyon and knew that the Great Salt Lake valley was where the saints would make our home.

On July twenty-fourth there would be a grand picnic in Pineridge, with races and games for the children. There would be a choir singing sacred songs and a procession of all the young saints as well as a reenactment of Brigham Young's historic vision. It was a time of great festivities and relaxation; the whole town looked forward to it.

Sister Cora always makes a trip to Moab beforehand to pick up special supplies for the picnic and the children's costumes. I usually accompany her to handle the exchange of money at Gentile businesses since I am good with numbers and Sister Cora stopped her schooling at the age of eleven. She always makes me double- and triple-check her change and receipts, since she says all Gentiles are liars and snakes.

When Mama told me I was to go into town the next day with Sister Cora, I knew that my chance had come. It would be perhaps the only one I had to get out of Pineridge.

The night before, I couldn't sleep, knowing that it would be my last with my family. Mama would see my escape as a final betrayal. But I had no choice. Once outside, I would find help. I could explain to the Gentiles that I was escaping a forced marriage that went against their laws. Maybe I would find Cliff, maybe he even knew where Joseph John was. That idea buoyed my spirits.

I put on both pairs of my sacred undergarments before bed so I could get dressed quickly in the morning. I wouldn't be able to bring anything else without alerting Sister Cora's suspicion but I knew my undergarments would be enough. They would protect me from danger and all manner of harm.

The time had come.

CHAPTER FOURTEEN

THE NEXT MORNING, I DID MY KITCHEN DUTIES with extra care, trying to memorize the scents, the sounds of home: my mother's profile as she pounded the bread dough, the whistling of the teakettle. As Sister Cora and I left for town, I said good-bye to my sisters casually but inside I was dying. Letting them go was harder than I thought. I noticed every detail of the house, the front porch, the lace curtains, things I had taken for granted every day and would surely miss.

Once in the car with Sister Cora, I stared out the window at the landscape, the patches of sego lilies, the pale pink and white yucca flowers amid the scrub brush and wild sage. I would never travel down this road again.

We pulled into Moab off highway 191, and as always Sister Cora parked the car in the lot located at the edge of town, where there were no meters requiring coins. I followed her down the sidewalk to the town center. A large banner hung across Main Street that said red rock music festival. There were more people than usual in town for the event and silently, I thanked God for this blessing. It would be easier to disappear.

On the streets of Moab, we stuck out in our long dresses and traditional hairstyles. Everyone else wore shorts and T-shirts, exposing their bodies in a shameful way. I could barely bring myself to look at them, but I told myself that I would have to get accustomed to it if I were going to live outside. After all, Brenda turned out to be as nice as pie and perhaps many of these people were just the same.

Music played from the cafés and shops; the town was bustling with people on bicycles and renting equipment for outdoor sports. Sister Cora paid the Gentiles no mind and kept her head held high and her face impassive as we entered the Sewing Time fabric store to pick up bric-a-brac for the Pioneer Day costumes. *Is there a way out?* A back door opened to an alley but it was behind a large counter for cutting fabric, manned by two salesgirls who were busy with customers. It would be impossible to sneak out past them. I helped Sister Cora with her purchases and promised myself there would be another chance.

Back on the street, I saw how the people, especially the tourists, stared at us and my hopes sank. How did I expect to disappear into the crowd in my long FLDS dress?

We walked by the central park, where stages were set up and drummers formed a circle. Some of them were Seed of Cain, mixed with everyone, and it looked like Brenda said, that people outside accepted them, that out here they were just like everybody else.

Sister Cora went into the Dollar Tree to pick souvenirs for the younger children. I followed obediently. As she wandered the aisles of the store, I hovered near the front door, watching the crowd. Sister Cora glanced at me crossly and I pretended to be interested in the festivities outside. It was not the festivities that caught my attention; it was the growing crowd of people. There were so many of them, all pressed up together. Maybe I *could* mix in with them?

Everything seemed to be moving in slow motion. Sister Cora turned her back to me, the music started, and the people outside began to dance. They formed a human chain, a spontaneous, undulating line that moved down Main Street en mass.

All I had to do was step into that crowd, step into a different world where people danced, women wore slacks, and no one could make you marry against your will. All I had to do was join them and let them carry me along. This was my chance, it would not come again. Fate had given me this opening, placing this sea of anonymous humanity right in front of me. Sister Cora was inspecting ceramic curios, unaware that I had inched out the doorway onto the sidewalk. It was time.

I took a deep breath and stepped off the curb, moving to the middle of the crush of people. I let myself be carried along a few feet and then moved to the other side of the group, bolting to cut across the park. Sister Cora would never see me even if she were looking, there were too many people blocking the way.

I darted down an alleyway behind shops and restaurants. The alley ended at a brick wall, a dead end. I hurried along, peering into each business I passed, looking for a place to hide. I slipped on a wet patch and stumbled, dirtying my dress on the grubby pavement. I saw the kitchen of a small café, the storage room of a bicycle shop, all busy with customers who would see me and notice my strange clothes. Suddenly I heard Sister Cora's voice, calling my name on the adjacent street. Soon she would give everyone my description and it would be impossible to get away. Desperate, I ducked into the next open doorway.

I found myself in the back room of a store that sold weavings, photographs, and other items I had never seen before: small glass pipes in different bright colors, tall cylindrical glasses that had an odd spout on one side. A curtain with a midnight blue pattern hung separating the back room from the rest of the shop where all manner of fabrics were folded and stacked. Where did these come from? I had never seen such an explosion of color and strange, beautiful designs in embroidery before.

At a glass case displaying the pipes, a man stood dressed in baggy white pants and a rainbow-colored vest. His hair was graying and worn in the same braids as the Seed of Cain drummers I had seen in the park. I had never seen a man dressed in such a way and I was afraid to approach him but I had to. Sister Cora would be coming down the alley looking for me at any moment.

"Excuse me," I said, and the man jumped and then broke into a laugh.

"Wow, you freaked me out! What's going on? Little early for Halloween, isn't it?" he asked, pointing to my dress and hair.

"I'm hiding from a lady who's looking for me, I can't let her find me, and—"

"Whoa, slow down," the man said. "You say you're hiding from someone? What's that about, is she bad news?"

"No—I mean yes, she is. She wants to take me back to Pineridge and I just escaped from there. . . ." I pointed to the back door, panicked that Sister Cora might burst through it at any moment.

The braided man moved toward me with a calming gesture and turned the bolt on the door to the alleyway. "Chill out, take a deep breath. See? You're safe in here."

Whoever this strange man was, at least he had kept Sister Cora from marching in the back door to grab me.

"So now, what's your story?" he asked, rolling a skinny cigarette on his knee.

Cigarettes and tobacco are forbidden in Pineridge; I had never seen someone smoking before. When he lit the cigarette, it gave off a pungent smoke. I wrinkled my nose. He waved the cigarette over his head with a smile. "Little ganja to start the day off right! So, tell me, what's your name?"

"Alva Jane."

He extended a hand with several large silver and turquoise rings on it. *A man wearing rings?* In Pineridge women wore only simple wedding bands and no man would be caught dead with rings on his fingers. But I wasn't in Pineridge anymore. I took his hand gingerly.

"I'm Jere," he said. "That's *J-E-R-E*. Used to be Jerry like Jerry Lewis, but I changed it to Jere when I moved here, got out of the rat race, you know? So, what's going on with you?" he asked, folding his arms over his chest.

"I've just escaped from Pineridge. We're FLDS."

"What the hell is that?"

"It's the Fundamentalist Church of the Latter Day Saints. You know, Mormons."

"Oh. Hell, sure are a lot of them here in Utah. Don't know how I missed that when I bought this shop. I'm from New York, originally. Used to be a stockbroker, can you imagine that? Me in a suit and tie every day?" He laughed loudly. I had no idea what he was talking about but nodded politely. I moved nearer to the door in case I had to run out and escape from him.

He continued, "Didn't I read something about that FL-whatever group in the newspaper? Isn't that the cult where you have to milk the cows and do tons of work and the men have a bunch of wives?" He took a long breath through his cigarette.

"Yes, I guess so," I said. I had certainly never met anyone like Jere but he was keeping me hidden from Sister Cora and as much as he scared me, Sister Cora scared me more. I couldn't risk leaving his shop.

"It sounded pretty intense. I can see why you'd want to get away from there. So, this lady who's looking for you wants to take you back. Is she your mom?"

"No, she's not. I need somewhere to hide until she leaves town. Can I wait here until I know she's gone?"

Jere waved me into the main shop and pulled up a chair for

me in a little room with its own door. "Sure, you can hang in the dressing room so no one sees you. I'm totally against all that kind of shit, you know? Establishment, rigid rules, structure. That's why I left Manhattan. You can hang here all day if you want. I have some cool *National Geographic*s in the back and a whole book of great photos."

He handed me a fat album filled with images of black-haired children and women wearing the bright-colored weavings he sold.

"Where are these from?" I asked.

"Guatemala. I lived down there for a few years. Now that is a crazy-ass country but they have amazing weavers. Look at this stuff! These women have been weaving these designs for, like, centuries. Each region has its own pattern so the Indians can identify each other. Great people, weird government . . ." He trailed off, busy unloading a new box of glass pipes.

I settled into the dressing room, looking through the book of photos at people I had never heard of, never seen. I thought of Cliff's words at school the day of Sister Emily's book burning. *There's a whole big world out there and they don't live like we do.*

And now I was in that world. I had done it! I had escaped the compound and all I had to do was wait until dark, when there was no chance of Sister Cora being in town to catch me.

It was well past midnight when I ventured out of Jere's shop. He was having what he called a salon, with a group of people talking about things I had never heard adults discuss: the president, a movie they had seen, a song by someone famous named Sting.

I'd stayed hidden in the back room but I had listened to every word they said.

When I left, Jere gave me a small box filled with tiny dolls dressed in brightly colored clothes. "These are Guatemalan worry dolls. When you've got a lot on your mind you put them under your pillow and they take your worries away. Good luck, Alva!"

Jere was the oddest man I had ever met and I knew he was the kind of person that the prophet had warned us about. But he had helped me, bought me lunch, and even given me the pretty little worry dolls. Whatever his sins, he was more good than bad and God had to see that.

On the street I saw a young couple walking arm in arm, laughing and talking. I imagined what it would be like to have such freedoms, to walk openly with a sweetheart, to wear modern clothes? Soon I would know.

A police car drove slowly toward me and I realized they might be the people to help. I waved my arms and the car stopped. An officer got out and looked me up and down, taking in my appearance.

"Can I help you, miss?" the officer asked. The name tag pinned to his uniform said oberg. He had thin hair and a large belly.

"My name is Alva Jane Merrill. I've run away from the FLDS in Pineridge, about an hour from here."

From inside the police car, a younger officer leaned over. "That's the little girl we were looking for, isn't it, Oberg?" he asked.

"Appears that way. Do you want to come down to the station with us, young lady, so we can take a statement?"

"Thank you, officer." I climbed into the back of the police car, relieved to be safely off the streets of the unfamiliar town. Officer Oberg asked how old I was.

"I'm fourteen, sir."

"Kind of young to be out on your own, aren't you?"

"Yes, sir, but I had to escape. My family was going to marry me against my will. And I have heard that there is an age-of-consent law."

The younger officer whistled, let out a chuckle, and said, "She's a smart one, that's for sure!"

When we arrived at the police station, Officer Oberg took me inside to a room with a chair and table. "I'll be back to take your statement in a moment, miss. Would you like some decaf? A Sprite maybe? There's herbal tea, too."

"No, thank you, sir." *They must be Mormons.* I knew because they had no caffeinated beverages and Uncle Kenton says that the Gentiles drink their weight in coffee and Coca-Cola every day, rotting their brains and their insides. That the officers were Mormons made me feel better. They would understand. Mainstream Mormons don't practice plural marriage, and I knew that they could be excommunicated from the LDS church if they were caught at it. But they knew the history of their own church. It would be easier to explain things to them than to Gentiles of a different religion altogether. I waited a long time for Officer Oberg to return. I thought that perhaps he had forgotten about me. Finally, he came back with an official-looking form. He sat across from me, drinking a Sprite.

"Okay, miss. So you say you're escaping a marriage that your family has arranged for you in Pineridge, is that right?"

"Yes, sir."

"And why are you opposed to getting married? Isn't that what all young girls want?"

His question surprised me. "Well, yes, I want to get married . . . but not to the person my parents want me to marry."

"But you're just a kid. You must have a crush on a boy from school or something, right?" He smiled at me in a way that made me uneasy. I didn't know how anything worked on the outside world but I didn't think this officer Oberg was supposed to be asking about Joseph John. But maybe he had seen him? Maybe he had picked up Joseph John after he was expelled?

"Have you seen a boy named Joseph John Hilliard? He was expelled from Pineridge a few weeks ago." Officer Oberg sat back in his chair drumming his fingers on his stomach, a wide grin spreading across his round face.

"So that's it, isn't it? Off chasing a bad boy who got himself kicked out?" His laugh made me even more nervous.

I wished the younger officer would come in. I didn't like Officer Oberg or the way he smiled at me. I squirmed; I hadn't used the restroom since before I left Pineridge.

"May I be excused to use the ladies' room, sir?"

"Of course, honey. It's right down the hall to the left."

I hurried to the bathroom. When I was done I looked at myself in the mirror and saw that my hair was disheveled, my dress stained from the fall in the dirty alleyway. I certainly didn't look respectable; perhaps that was why Officer Oberg had questioned me that way. I did my best to straighten my hair out and smooth my dress into place. I walked back to the interview room, hoping that the other officer might have come in. When I opened the door, I saw that Officer Oberg was still there. But someone new had arrived. My mother and father sat stiffly, awaiting my return.

CHAPTER FIFTEEN

THE NEXT MOMENTS WERE A BLUR, FACING MY parents and the realization that the police had called them to come for me. The officers were supposed to protect me, but they were delivering me back into the hands of the very people I was trying to escape from. Mama grabbed hold of my arm and Daddy shook hands with Officer Oberg, who said, "Do you know Leon Knast? Is he still living out in Pineridge? He's my second cousin on my dad's side."

He's FLDS. He lives out here but he's part of it!

My parents led me to the car in silence. I was afraid to even look at them. Once they started driving, my father said quietly, "You've broken my heart, Alva Jane. Broken it into a million pieces. I never expected this from you, not from you of all my daughters."

My father's disappointment stung me but I could not find any words to speak.

He continued, "And you should have known that the police and other people out here aren't going to help you. Did you hear that officer? He's Leon Knast's cousin. You know how many mainstream Mormons living on the outside have ties to the FLDS? How many of them go along with the apostates but know in their hearts that the day of reckoning will come when all will be made right, and plural marriage will be the law of the land for God's chosen people? They're not going to help you leave the flock, Alva. In time you'll thank heaven that man did right by calling us. But for now . . ." His voice broke off.

I feared what he would say next, what my punishment might be for such a grave offense. Surely the prophet had been told, surely my trespass was known to all. And surely there would be serious consequences.

"I just didn't know what else to do, Daddy," I began, but my mother cut me off.

"The time for explanations is over, Alva. And no more of your lies, either. Leigh Ann told her husband today how you lied to keep your cycle a secret. Like a good priesthood man, he came directly to your father, who had to endure the shame of having your deceit exposed in such a way!"

I started to shake. It seemed the whole world was working against me. They knew the truth. Leigh Ann had betrayed me. My escape had failed. I was being taken back to a life I knew I could not bear.

Outside the car the desert faded into blackness just beyond

the high-beam lights. I wished I could be swallowed up into that abyss of darkness. Anything to escape the punishment that awaited me at home.

Daddy drove in silence for a few minutes and then turned to Mama in the backseat with me. "Two of your children have disgraced our family in a matter of weeks, Maureen. Do you have any idea how this will look to the prophet? He could take serious steps against me, against our family!"

"They are not just my children, Eldon Ray. They are yours as well."

"None of my others have behaved this way!"

"What about Sister Cora's boys? The first Eldon Ray Jr. and Lamont? They both left Pineridge," Mama dared to point out.

"They left on their own, they were not expelled. And none of the girls have tried to escape this way. There is something in your bloodline that brings out this disobedience. It has nothing to do with me!" he snapped.

With that, Mama held her tongue.

Then Daddy said, "When we return, I want you to move from the main house to one of the trailers with the older children. Cora will take charge of the twins, Carlene, Lucy, Marcus, and baby Rowena. They are young enough, they still have a chance to escape being corrupted."

I could not believe what my father was saying! Mama would lose not only her place in the house but her children?

My mother's face was drained of all color. "But Eldon Ray, they are my babies!"

But Daddy would hear none of it. "It's been decided. You

will take Sister Marcie's trailer. She will take your rooms in the house and share them with the smallest children, who will remain. Perhaps this will cleanse the spirit of rebellion that they have inherited from you."

Mama fought back angry tears and whispered, "This is Cora's doing isn't it? This isn't about Alva or Cliff, it's about Sister Marcie and you wanting to have her close by. It was the same with me, wasn't it? When I joined the family and Sherrie was pushed out?"

"Be quiet, woman, I won't have you talking against any other sister wives with your poisonous jealousy. Cora is right about you. Thank heaven she showed me the error of my ways."

Mama said no more. We turned into the main gates of Pineridge as the sky was beginning to break to pale gray. We pulled up outside the house and my father said, "Put her in one of the hideaways. I don't want the other children to see her."

With that he disappeared up the stairway to Sister Cora's room. The house was quiet when Mama led me inside. The hideaways were hidden compartments built into the walls of the house. Almost every FLDS home had them to hide multiple wives and children in case of sudden police raids and investigations. I had been in one when I was small and there was talk of a raid that had never happened. I'd hidden in there with Mama and Cliff; we were her only two children at that time. The hideaways were dark and cramped but safe from prying eyes.

Mama took me to a hideaway on the second floor, opened the door, and waited, wiping her tears with the back of her hand. "This is all your fault, Alva Jane. I warned you that we could all suffer, and your only thought was of yourself. Get inside," she ordered.

I knelt and climbed in. My heart broke for my siblings who would leave the main house to live in the trailers, out of favor with our father. But I was not to blame for Daddy's change of heart. I'd heard what Mama said in the car. It wasn't about Cliff or me, it was about Sister Marcie, whose trailer Daddy had been visiting every night. It was about all the things Mama had predicted and feared with a new young wife in the fold, the things I hadn't wanted to believe about my father.

I sat against the wall, my knees drawn up underneath me. My mother closed the door behind me and I heard a latch slide into place. I tried to open the door and found that it was bolted shut from the outside.

The outside? Why on earth would a hideaway have a lock on the outside?

I began to panic. There was no way out! I listened to my mother's footsteps disappear. What if they left me inside forever, a disgrace to the family better to be forgotten? I did not sleep. When the sun came up and a thin ray of light filtered in through the wooden lathe to the hallway, I saw writing scratched into the wall of the hideaway. The words read, help me. i am sherrie.

Sister Sherrie, my father's third wife, who hardly spoke and was afraid of her own shadow, who lived alone in the converted shed out back? Sister Sherrie, who had been pushed out when Mama joined the family, like she said in the car before Daddy silenced her. Had sister Sherrie been locked up here once as well?

My father built this house; there were no prior inhabitants. If Sister Sherrie or anyone else had been locked up in here against her will, it had been Daddy's doing.

What kind of man was my father? He was the sun that our family orbited around. He was always ready with a grin and a slap on the back, secure in his role as the prophet's right hand. But now that he was afraid of losing Uncle Kenton's confidence, he was showing a different face altogether.

I had seen him the way a small child would, believing in his easy smile and the little trinkets he had handed out to his favorite children, the extra piece of pie, the prettiest fabric for a new dress. Who was he that he could cast a favored wife aside so easily and take her children from her? That he could lock up a daughter in this dark hole? What else was he capable of? What other secrets did this house hold?

I thought back to my punishment in the barn, the uncontrollable fury that overtook him, the way his hand dripped with sweat when it was over, and how Mama held me still to receive the blows from his belt. I thought I knew them. But now I saw that I did not, that I never had.

The realization hit me like a blow to the stomach, but unlike the whipping in the barn, this time I did not cry. The time for tears was past. Every face I loved and trusted belonged to a stranger, an enemy. Their love for me was not love at all but something else. I was just a pawn in my father's quest to secure his position with Uncle Kenton and, in turn, a playing piece in Mama's plan to regain Daddy's favor.

The pain of this truth hurt more than anything else. Worse

than the beating with Daddy's belt, worse than the silence, than being shut out of my family. It was as if I had been ripped away from a part of myself. It was betrayal, knowing that everything I believed in had been false. Above all, I knew that my survival was in my own hands. But for now, my life was in theirs.

All day I stayed locked up in the hideaway, unable to move. I had no water, no food, even when the midday heat rose. Maybe they hoped that I would die in there and make everything easy for them. It was well after bedtime when I heard Mama's footsteps in the hallway and the door jerked open. My bladder was about ready to burst and I ran to the bathroom to keep from wetting myself. When I came out, Daddy stood with Mama at the top of the stairs and said the words I dreaded to hear.

"The prophet wants to see you now."

CHAPTER SIXTEEN

I STOOD IN THE PROPHET'S OFFICE, LINED WITH photos of former FLDS leaders and a large drawing of Brigham Young. My parents had forbidden me to change my clothes, so I still wore my stained dress from my trip to Moab. I felt dirty and ashamed facing the most powerful man in Pineridge in such condition.

My mother and father stood beside me, ready to hear the prophet's judgment. Uncle Kenton rose from his desk and stood to face me, his hands folded in front of him. "So, you tried to escape your marriage, to escape the community that nurtured you, loved you, and provided you with a clear and easy path to the celestial kingdom. Can you tell me why, Alva Jane? Why you have rejected God's love and his plan for you?"

I was too intimidated to speak directly to the prophet, I didn't know how to explain myself now that he was standing right in front of me. My reasons for leaving seemed weak and immature compared to God's plan for me. I looked at my dusty shoes and said nothing.

"And you, Eldon Ray, how can it be that two of your children have shown such disobedience in such a short time? Aren't you in control of your household?" Uncle Kenton asked.

"Yes, I am, Uncle Kenton. I have taken steps to root out this rebellion that comes from Maureen's family line. Today she was moved from the main house with the older children to one of the trailers out back. Sister Marcie, your niece, has been moved inside the main house to help Cora care for the younger children and protect them from this inheritance."

"Perhaps Marcie will prove to be more reliable in bringing up righteous offspring, willing to accept God's wisdom," Uncle Kenton said with a sharp glance at Mama, who kept her eyes on the floor. He turned his attention back to me.

"As for you, young lady, you need a firm hand and the stability of marriage to bring you to heel. Your heart is in the wrong place and it must be made right. My brother Wade has generously agreed to go ahead with his marriage to you, despite your disobedience. You should count yourself lucky that any Pineridge man will have you after your behavior, but my brother is forgiving and righteous in his service to God."

Uncle Kenton moved to the door of his office and opened it, ushering in Wade Barton. Panic took hold of me. I was trapped in this room, with my parents behind me, the prophet before me, and the man they intended to marry me to waiting, ready. There was no way out.

"I'm going to perform the sealing ceremony right here. I think it prudent not to take any more chances with Miss Alva Jane," Uncle Kenton said.

I felt sick and dizzy. Here, in the middle of the night, in a filthy dress with no ceremony, no celebration, I would begin my life as the sixth wife of a man I felt nothing but fear and revulsion for.

"Brother Wade, please take Sister Alva's right hand in the patriarchal grip," the prophet began.

"Do you, Brother Wade Barton, take Sister Alva Jane Merrill by the right hand and receive her unto yourself to be your lawful and wedded wife and you to be her lawful and wedded husband for time and all eternity?"

"I do."

"And do you, Sister Alva Jane Merrill, take Brother Wade Barton by the right hand and give yourself to him of your own free will and choice?"

Uncle Kenton's words hung in the air. I wanted to scream, *This is not my will!* They all knew it, yet they stood before God and lied. And they wanted me to lie also. I could not speak although everyone was waiting for my response. I felt my mother's hand on my back, prodding me.

Mama leaned in and whispered, "Be strong. Trust in the Lord."

Uncle Kenton repeated the vow, forcefully.

Finally I whispered, "I do."

"Now go forth and replenish the earth with good priesthood children. May you be fruitful and multiply," Uncle Kenton said with a satisfied smile.

I couldn't bring myself to look at my new husband. Uncle Kenton told him to kiss the bride and I felt Wade's thick lips pressing against mine. I closed my mouth, tightly. The whole thing was over so quickly. My fate was sealed.

My parents thanked the prophet for his forgiveness and generosity. They thanked Brother Wade for saving me from ruin and perdition. Daddy held my hand in his and said, "You'll see, Alva. This is for the best. You have to trust your parents and the prophet."

Mama smoothed my hair into place and whispered, "Keep sweet, Alva, above all."

The prophet yawned. "You may use one of the bedrooms on the basement floor for your wedding night, Brother Wade. You don't want to disturb your household at this hour, not with Sister LeNan so close to giving birth."

"Thank you, Kenton," Brother Wade said, taking me by the hand and leading me into the darkened hallway, down the stairway to the lowest level of the house. The walls of Uncle Kenton's mansion were thick limestone. It was like a fortress with many rooms below the ground level, secret meeting rooms for the councilmen, for special ceremonies. It was in one of these impenetrable rooms that Sister Ann Marie had received her discipline for the same offense that I had committed, at the hand of the husband that we now shared.

Brother Wade led me into a room furnished with nothing more than an overhead light and a bed covered in a faded spread. I stood unmoving in the middle of the room.

"We must consummate the marriage and I must make you my wife in every sense of the word, Alva Jane," he said, a sly pleasure creeping into his voice. I said nothing.

"You tried to escape and I don't take kindly to that, as you know. But I'm going to give you the benefit of the doubt and believe that it was just the anxieties of a young girl, fearful of fulfilling her obligations to her husband."

He stepped toward me and I instinctively stepped away. He advanced slowly, backing me toward the bed until I felt my legs pressed against it.

"Please, Brother Wade," I said.

"I'm your husband now, not Brother Wade." He inched even closer still, his breath on me. He grabbed my wrists suddenly, pulling me off balance, and with a quick shove he pushed me onto my back on the bed. In a moment he was on top of me, his body pinning me down.

I was terrified of what was about to happen. His weight on top of me was suffocating and I tried to squirm away but he laid a thick forearm against my neck and held my face toward him. With his other hand he roamed over my dress, feeling the form of my body. I felt a scream rising in my throat but he sensed it and he put his heavy hand across my mouth.

"You don't want to wake the prophet and his household, Alva Jane. Not when I am just taking what is rightfully mine," he whispered, his breath hot against my neck. He groped my breast and when he found the nipple through the fabric of my bodice he caught it between two knuckles and pinched it hard. I cried out in pain, it hurt so much. He smiled then, and pressed his lips against mine. I saw that he enjoyed hurting me, he enjoyed my fear. I used all my strength to try to get out from under him but he held me fast.

"Stop trying to get away; you are doing your duty as my wife," he growled as he began pulling up my dress. He pushed it over my knees and up around my thighs and then he began reaching, pulling at my sacred undergarments. I had never felt so sinful, so mortified.

I began to cry. "Please don't," I begged.

He had my undergarments down around my calves. I was shamefully naked with his sweating body pressed against mine.

"You must submit to me as your husband, Alva Jane," he said, forcing his mouth over mine and sticking his tongue inside it. I gagged.

I coughed for air as Wade pulled back to open his pants. In a moment he was atop me again, but now I felt something hard pressing against my leg. I moved away but Wade pressed his forearm against my throat, making it hard to breathe. I stopped squirming for fear that he would strangle me right there. Then he took my hand and pushed it down between his legs, forcing me to touch his privates. He held my hair in his grip, and I could not move while he whispered things in my ear, disgusting, vile things that it was sinful to even think on.

This is wrong, this cannot be right!

I tried to tune his voice out, to think of anything else, but my mind was blank. I thought it could get no worse when suddenly I felt his legs pushing my knees apart. In the next moment Wade pushed himself inside me. The pain was so great, it felt as if he were tearing me apart. I cried out, begging him to stop.

"Good girl," he whispered in my ear as he pounded his body into me with a fury that I was sure would split me in two.

Please, God, let me die rather than endure this!

I cried openly, my tears running down my neck and onto my dirty dress. I pleaded with Wade to stop, but he kept on for what seemed like an eternity, enjoying my suffering, excited by my cries of pain. Surely the others in the house could hear me. Someone would come to my aid. But no one came.

Finally, with a loud groan, he finished and rolled away. I felt something warm and sticky running down my thigh. I felt violated, broken beyond repair. I could not stop crying. My throat was raw when I turned my face into the bedspread in shame.

This is wrong, so wrong. Surely this is not what my parents, the prophet, or God intended!

Wade stood and did up his pants. "Put yourself together, you look a mess," he said. "We have to walk back to our house now."

My legs wobbled when I stood. I ran a hand over my hair, now messy and knotted. I saw the fresh bloodstain on my undergarments when I tried to put them on properly.

"I'm bleeding!" I cried.

But Wade laughed at my terror.

"All women bleed the first time. At least it proves that your young sweetheart didn't get to you first. Come on." He grabbed my arm and led me out into the hallway. My legs felt like rubb
when I walked. I stuck my hand into the pocket of my felt the small box of worry dolls that Jere had given me, a little talisman of the hopes that were now destroyed. My mother's final admonishment played back in my head.

Keep sweet, Alva Jane, above all.

We stepped out into the cool night air to walk the block to Wade's house. I lost my footing on the pathway and felt his hand on my shoulder, roughly pulling me upright. We arrived and he held the front door to the house open.

"Welcome to your new home," he said.

My head felt light and the scene began to spin wildly. Then the blackness fell over me.

CHAPTER SEVENTEEN

I awoke in the same basement room where I had tended to Sister Ann Marie. There were no windows, no outside light. My stained dress was crumpled on the floor and I lay in bed in nothing but my torn undergarments. In the room above I heard footsteps, muffled voices. I got up stiffly, flinching at the pain between my legs. I wanted to bathe, to wash away all signs of the nightmare I had lived through. I heard the door to the basement open and Sister Irene came down the stairs.

"Time to get up, Sister Alva. It's past ten o'clock. I let you sleep in today, last night being your wedding night. But now it's time to get to work. The devil loves idle hands. You're to clean the bathrooms, top to bottom. The toilet bowls, the bathtubs, the sinks. The vinegar and water are upstairs in a bucket."

"Is there a bathroom I can use? I need to clean up and get dressed properly."

"I can see that. Your mother dropped off all of your clothes early this morning and I put them in that cabinet. This will be your room; the upstairs bedrooms are full. You can wash up in the bath by the laundry room. Hurry up, we've lots to do today." And she left, her shoes clicking against the wooden floor.

I found the laundry room, washed up, and got dressed. I moved like a zombie; I felt half-alive. Then I went to work on the bathrooms. As I scrubbed the first toilet bowl, Sister Ann Marie walked by slowly, leaning on a willow cane with a pile of folded laundry balanced in her arms. She looked at me with no sign of recognition and kept going.

The house was deadly quiet, except for the sound of a mop swishing in the stairwell, a baby crying somewhere upstairs. If there were children in the house, they were as quiet as mice. Sister LeNan walked by with a large bucket of water, trying to stay upright despite her enormous pregnant belly.

"Hi, Sister Alva, welcome to the family. I'm doing the kitchen," she said warmly. I couldn't help staring at her huge abdomen, counting back the weeks since I last saw her.

"Isn't your baby due already, LeNan?"

LeNan blushed and dropped her voice. "It was supposed to come almost three weeks ago, but Sister Irene said with the change in the season, babies sometimes wait."

She patted her stomach happily and whispered, "The best thing is that when you're pregnant, your husband can't have any sex with you. It's too bad for the other sister wives, but it's been

176

nice for me. But soon, it will be back to normal." She sighed and disappeared with the bucket.

Three little girls walked down the hallway, holding hands, whispering so quietly they seemed like ghosts. They looked at me fearfully and hurried past. Clearly everyone in this family was afraid of something, and it wasn't hard to figure out who it was. I turned back to scrubbing the white tile of the bath-tub. My body ached, my hands shook, and my eyes kept spilling over with tears no matter how hard I willed them to stop. One thought played over and over in my head.

I cannot fall apart. I must stay focused. I have to get out of this house, out of Pineridge, no matter the consequences.

CHAPTER EIGHTEEN

AT THE END OF THE DAY I WAS EXHAUSTED FROM work but it felt good to have done something, anything, to keep my mind occupied. All day long I imagined different escape plans. I would not be so naive as I had been the last time. I would not get caught and be brought back again; I would die first.

At dinner I sat between Brother Wade and Sister Irene and it was clear that all the sister wives knew of my attempted escape and were keeping a close eye on me. Unlike at my family's home, Wade's sister wives did not seem to be in competition for his favor. They shared a mute solidarity against a common cross they all had to bear. But despite the sense that they understood my suffering, I knew that my sister wives obeyed their priesthood head, they did what Wade told them to do. They would not help my escape.

I was not allowed outside the house and the only time I was unaccompanied was when I was cleaning and there was a sister wife in the next room. They were taking no chances with me. When I went down to my basement bedroom, Sister Irene locked me in. I was a prisoner in my new home, my marriage. With nothing else to do, I sat on the bed, laying out my strategy for escape. I would learn everything I could about the household routine, when Wade was gone, what he did each day. There had to be a way out and I would find it.

I would be vigilant and single-minded. Anything less felt like an acceptance of my fate and I knew that would kill me. I could not become like Sister Sherrie, a faint shadow of a woman living on half rations of life. I would never accept this fate, married to a monster like Wade Barton. I heard the door latch open and footsteps on the basement stairs. Wade appeared, leaning against the stairwell, casting an appraising eye over me.

I said nothing, hoping for the best and fearing the worst.

"A new wife whets a man's appetite for certain things," he said, moving toward me.

I braced myself for what I knew would come next and prayed to a merciful God that it would be over soon.

For three weeks I remained sequestered in Wade's house. I had no visitors. I went outside only to hang the wash to dry with Sister Irene. To anyone in Pineridge, it would appear that I had simply disappeared. My previous life, attending the Zion Academy, working in the Pineridge store with Mr. Battle, stood in stark contrast to the narrow confines of my life as Wade's sixth wife. I knew I had to find a way to loosen the grip of my imprisonment, to have contact outside of the Barton household, if I ever hoped to escape.

Every night Wade descended the steps into my windowless room and took full advantage of what he called his rights as a husband. He did things to me that were an abomination before God, things that I knew must be prohibited and sinful. But I had no recourse, no one to turn to for help. When my cycle came in the first week of my marriage, he was supposed to stay away from me until it ended, but he did not, defying the rules of The Principle.

He was trying to break my spirit as well as my body, to bring me to heel as Uncle Kenton had said that fateful night of our wedding. But I sensed that all of my sister wives suffered the same way, that his aggression was rooted in something deep in his character, something angry that enjoyed humiliation, that thrilled at causing pain.

I'd seen it the night of Ann Marie's discipline. I saw it every night when he forced himself upon me in degrading ways. I developed a way of disassociating from these encounters, willing my mind elsewhere, withdrawing completely from what was taking place. It was my only way of holding onto my sanity. Afterward I felt dirty and embarrassed. Late each night when the household was asleep, I snuck into the laundry room bath and turned the water on as hot as I could stand it, trying to scald the shame from my skin.

On Pioneer Day, the sister wives and children attended the celebration but I was not allowed to go. Sister Irene locked me into my basement room. I thought I was alone in the house until

I heard the distinctive shuffling of Ann Marie's feet and the tap-tap-tap of her cane as she came down the hallway. She stopped at the top of the stairs. Then I heard the doorway latch being undone.

"Alva Jane?"

"I'm down here!" I rushed to the bottom of the stairs. Ann Marie had not so much as looked me in the eye since my arrival but now she stood at the top of the stairway, seeking me out.

"If I go down I may have trouble getting back up with this bad leg. If they catch us talking, he'll kill us both," she whispered.

"Did they lock you in too?"

"They used to, but since I need help walking, they thought it was safe to leave me alone. You have to try to get away again, Alva. If you don't you'll be stuck here forever. I can't do it now, but you still can!"

Was this a setup, a way of getting me to talk about my escape plan and then tell Wade? Had he ordered Ann Marie to seek me out and gain my confidence? It sounded insane but I couldn't take any chances. I said nothing, waiting for Ann Marie to continue.

"I'll help you any way I can," she offered.

"Why? If you can't get away?"

"Because if you do, you can tell them what's going on in here. Maybe someone will come to help all of us."

"And how am I going to escape? I'm trapped, they never let me out of here!"

"They can't keep you locked up forever. I'll see if I can piece together the things you'll need, like clothes, water, and food."

I still had arms and legs that could run, I had eyes that could see. I had abilities that she no longer had, and her hopes were pinned on me.

Outside, a car backfired. Ann Marie flinched. "I can't stay, they could come back at any moment. I have something for you. I never got to use it. It's hidden behind the armoire, in the cinder block. Look for the chipped piece."

She walked away, her cane thumping against the wooden floor. I went to the heavy armoire and pulled it away from the wall, all the while listening for the sound of the family returning. I ran my hands over the cinder block and found a chipped corner piece. I pulled the block out and reached inside the hollow center. It was a small plastic bag containing a wad of bills, a slim box of used eye shadow, and a tube of store-bought hair dye.

Where had she gotten these things? The Pineridge store didn't sell such items. And what good were makeup and hair dye to me? Maybe her discipline had addled Ann Marie's brain as well as her body. Then I realized that she was sharper than I had given her credit for. To escape successfully I would have to change the way I looked once I was outside the compound walls. I would have to change everything about myself to avoid being caught. I would leave behind the horrors of my marriage, my family, even my identity.

If Ann Marie could find hope somewhere within her broken body, then so could I. And count myself lucky that I had not yet met the same fate.

That evening the tension in the house was thicker than usual. I was able to piece together that the Pioneer Day celebrations had not gone well. The prophet had been tense and argumentative, even with his Priesthood Council. Since my arrival in the house, I had heard the whispered conversations between Sister Irene and Wade, the footsteps of men coming in the back door for late-night meetings. Something was afoot in Pineridge.

After Wade left my room that night, I was unable to sleep. I sat in the dark and thought about all the things I had seen and accepted over the years. Alone in the dark, my doubts grew into disbelief. Beyond the loss of faith in my parents I saw shadows of the reality that was hidden behind their devotion to the Brotherhood. My punishment, Sister Sherrie's scrawled plea for help, and my mother's fall from grace upon Marcie Barton's arrival had shown me what was true and what was false. The questions I battled with multiplied. After that long night in the hideaway when first stones fell from the foundation upon which my life had been built, now the walls began to crumble and come down.

Keep sweet.

How many times had I been told that and how many times had I taken it to heart?

Keeping sweet was not for the good of my spirit, my soul, or for God. It was for the good of the prophet, the council, and the men who controlled our lives. How had keeping sweet helped my mother? It was obedience they wanted. And power. The power to keep a quorum of wives living in God's brothel, believing that their servitude was sanctified. I realized that I was a woman, no longer a girl in any sense of the word, and no longer an innocent.

The realization did not hit like a bolt of lightning from the sky. It happened slowly, eroding the outer layers of my beliefs, cutting away at the lies I had been fed, each painful snip taking a small piece of my soul. Until what was left was hard and brilliant, unbreakable, a diamond from a black lump of coal.

Now I saw it all clearly. Over the past few months, Uncle Kenton had become increasingly erratic and punitive, decreeing that there would be new rationing of water, a ban on the use of sugar, and other inexplicable regulations. His paranoia had been building, affecting even his closest followers. That was why Cliff had been expelled for such a small offense, why Ann Marie's attempted escape triggered the book burning and the prophet's sermons being played in all public places.

My father had given everything to the Brotherhood but now he was struggling financially, being sent away to Arizona regularly, and missing Priesthood Council decisions. Even his authority over his family was being questioned. That was why he had been so moody, so easily angered. And that was why I had been sacrificed in a marriage to a monster. To appease Uncle Kenton and win back his capricious favor.

Nothing was going right in Pineridge, the well-maintained order was slipping and the flock of followers, indoctrinated into unquestioning obedience, did not know what to do. In this growing chaos, I knew I had a chance. The idea came to me in the dead of night, with nothing to keep me company but my own desperation.

I knew that obedience and devotion mattered most to my parents and the prophet. I would use their belief against them. I would become the perfect, penitent sister wife, regain the trust that they needed so badly to reaffirm in these troubled times. I would be the prodigal daughter come home. And when they least suspected it, I would run.

CHAPTER NINETEEN

THE NEXT AFTERNOON AS I PASSED ANN MARIE IN the hallway, she handed me a basket of clean sheets to fold. "There are some extra buttons for the boys' shirts in the sewing box in your room, Sister Alva, and I'll need them to finish up the mending."

She gave me a pointed look and an insistent push.

I turned to Sister Irene, who was wiping down the walls with a wet sponge. "May I go downstairs to retrieve the buttons, Sister Irene?" I had to ask permission for everything, even the smallest tasks.

"Yes. The boys need those clothes mended before they go out to the fields to work."

"I'll get right to it." I went downstairs, taking the basket of linens with me. I rifled through the sheets to find a pair of boy's pants and a faded work shirt. I held them up; they looked as if they would fit. I hid them beneath my dresses and returned upstairs to work with a nod to Ann Marie. Together we would sneak and pilfer what was necessary. It felt good to have an ally in that quiet, menacing house.

That evening at dinner we ate in silence, the way we did everything in the Barton house. Once everyone had been served, I placed my hand lightly on Wade's arm and asked, "May I speak to the family, Wade?"

I could see he was puzzled but he agreed and I stood, looking around the table at my five sister wives, and the children seated at a long folding table nearby.

"I know that all of you know of my attempted escape from Pineridge and how our husband generously forgave me and accepted me as his sixth wife. . . ."

Sister Irene exchanged a look with Wade, who held his fork in midair as he listened. Ann Marie stared at me, uncertainty in her eyes. I met her stare evenly as I continued, "I know that I have broken the trust of the community and of my family and I ask your forgiveness. I realize now that my highest calling is to serve and obey my husband in all things, to accept his dominion over me, and to keep sweet at all times. I know it will take time and work to regain your trust, but I hope you will find it in your hearts to give me a chance. Thank you for letting me speak, Wade."

I squeezed Wade's arm and took Sister Irene's hand as I sat down.

"Those are fine words of repentance, Alva Jane. I'm very

happy to see this change in you, as we all are," Sister Irene said tersely, and Wade nodded in agreement. I resumed eating my dinner, my eyes humbly downcast. I stole a sideways glance at Ann Marie, who bit her lip to hold back a faint smile.

The next day I had a visitor; my mother showed up after breakfast bearing the gift of a new knitted shawl. Her eyes were brimming with joy as we sat in the kitchen, Mama's hand lovingly placed over mine.

"Sister Irene told me last night of your repentance, Alva. Your father and I could not be happier. We knew that once you were living within the bonds of celestial marriage you would recover yourself and become the obedient girl we have always loved."

I smiled. "You're right, Mama, like always." I knew exactly what to say and how to say it. I had spent a lifetime learning this role and now my life depended on playing it well.

"I just count myself lucky that my husband forgave my wickedness and independence," I added.

Mama reached out and smoothed my hair. "You look good, Alva. Marriage agrees with you."

My mother was a bad liar. I had seen my reflection in the mirror, I looked terrible. The strain of my life with Wade had drained all the color from me. The sleepless nights had etched deep circles under my eyes. But I also knew that Mama would believe what she wanted to believe; that was how she had survived all these years, and I would use that belief to my advantage. I took her hand.

"Mama, do you think Daddy could do me a favor? Could

he help arrange a meeting for me with Uncle Kenton? I want to make it right with him. To tell him firsthand that I have repented in my heart."

"I'm sure Daddy can do that for you, Alva. It would please him to no end. Things have been . . . difficult for your father and for all of us. But I take this change in you as a sign of a new day. My little girl has put her heart in the right place where God intended it to be and perhaps your father's heart will be moved to bring us back to the main house again.

"I have to get back to start the washing," Mama said, rising to go. At the door she leaned in close and whispered, "And there is big news! Rita Mae's daughter Marianne has been chosen to be the prophet's next wife! You know she's special, she always has been. It is such an honor for the family."

I didn't know how to respond. Marianne would be eleven years old next month; Uncle Kenton was old enough to be her grandfather. Of course she was special—she was mentally slow and timid, afraid of her own shadow. How could beautiful, sweet Marianne be expected to understand what marriage meant or what would be required of her? My stomach turned at the thought of a child facing what I was living through with Wade. I searched my mother's face for some recognition that this was an abomination, but there was none. Mama wore an expectant smile, waiting for my reply.

"That's wonderful, Mama. I hope that Daddy is pleased by it," I said, feeling the words thick in my throat.

"Well, you know Rita Mae was against it at first, her being so young and all. But your Daddy convinced her. After all,

Marianne isn't quite right; what if she doesn't get chosen for marriage by someone else? This way she is sure to be exalted, being married to the prophet."

I watched my mother walk away, knowing that she was untroubled by doubt. She was at peace with her unwavering devotion to The Principle no matter how twisted it became under Uncle Kenton's unstable hand. And I knew that I could not let Marianne be married off to the sixty-seven-year-old prophet. The family was in favor of it, there was no one else willing or ready to defend a helpless little girl. My escape plan had just become more complicated. It would now include a ten-year-old girl. I would take Marianne with me when I left.

In the weeks that followed, I rose early every day and helped Sister Irene above and beyond my assigned chores. I was tired and achy but kept going, determined to prove my new commitment to my husband and family. I baked extra bread, I scrubbed the canning jars, I took on extra sewing from Sister LeNan, who had finally given birth to her baby.

I did my best to appear willing toward Wade's advances but it still made my skin crawl when he touched me. I closed my eyes and imagined a life outside of Pineridge, living in a new place, with different people who knew nothing of my past. A clean slate, a new beginning, a new identity. That was the one thought that kept me alive every day.

Finally, Sister Irene asked me to accompany her to the Pineridge store to help her with purchases. Walking outside in the open air, I felt restored. The town looked the same except that new construction was underway at the temple with trucks coming and going steadily.

"Why so many trucks, Sister Irene?"

"The prophet is building two new turrets at the main gate, to keep us safe."

"Are the drivers Pineridge men? I don't recognize all of them."

"Most are, but there are some outsiders who come in and out with no dillydallying. We can't allow any of them to corrupt our community by mixing with the people here. The overseers are in charge of that."

I saw Jack Norton directing a group of men to unload a large flatbed filled with rebar. I took note of the trucks, the coming and going of deliveries. Perhaps there would be a way to use all that hustle and bustle to my benefit.

At the Pineridge store, Mr. Battle greeted me warmly, taking my hand in his.

"I guess you've been so busy with married life you've had no time to come by and visit old Mr. Battle," he said with a smile, and I felt a pang of remorse for what I knew I had to do.

Sister Irene gave me a list of items to find while she looked at fabrics. I moved through the familiar aisles, picking out Sister Irene's items and sneaking a few things for myself into the deep pockets of my dress. I knew stealing from Mr. Battle was wrong, but I had to get what I would need to survive on the outside: small scissors, a pocketknife, a flashlight.

After dinner, my parents came by to give me the good news that the prophet had granted me an audience before the Priesthood Council. He would receive me that very evening. I changed into my best dress. I arranged my hair neatly and stared at myself in the mirror. I looked like a perfect FLDS wife. I knew that convincing Uncle Kenton that I had repented was the key to everything. With his support I would be restored to the community and regain some measure of my freedom.

As we walked to the prophet's house, I rested my hand in the crook of Wade's arm, fighting the revulsion that his presence provoked in me. Just the scent of him made me ill, but I masked it beneath a submissive smile.

My father chattered as we walked. "I'm so happy you've had this change of heart, Alva. I was really worried about your soul that night we went to pick you up in Moab. You could have gone down a dangerous path, but a righteous husband and marriage have made you whole again!"

"Yes, Daddy."

I watched his broad back in front of me as he walked ahead. I looked at his head with its short haircut, like a black brush sitting stiff and upright, the back of his leathery neck burned a faint pink by the sun. My heart that had once been so filled with pride at the sight of him felt cold and hard inside as I watched him now. Like flashes of lightning I saw him raising his belt over me in the livestock barn, ordering Mama to give her children to Sister Cora, standing mutely by while I was married to a man he had seen beat a young wife senseless. I remembered his absence when we abandoned Cliff by the side of the road; he was not man enough to say good-bye to his own son or defend him. My father was no longer the priesthood head who would lead his family to exaltation but a coward, a blind follower, ready to sacrifice his children. I hated him now and the depth of the rancor in my heart surprised me.

At the prophet's home we were led to one of the conference rooms where the council met. I saw Tom Pruitt, Leroy Jaynes, and Eddie Raynard among them; they were councilmen come to weigh in on my fate. My father and Wade took their seats beside the prophet and I stepped forward. My blood pounded loudly, a steady drumbeat in my ears. I would give the performance of my life; I had to. I waited obediently for Uncle Kenton to grant me permission to speak.

"You've asked for an audience, Sister Alva, after some grievous trespasses against my authority and the community. My brother tells me that you have repented, is that true?"

I took a deep breath and prayed for strength. "Yes, Uncle Kenton. I have repented for my wickedness and disobedience. I now see that you and my parents know what is best for me and being married to a righteous man like Brother Wade is exactly what the Lord intended for me."

Uncle Kenton squinted his eyes at me warily. I knew it would be harder to convince him than it had been my parents. "And what brought on this sudden change of heart, after such a brazen escape attempt?"

"I don't know exactly. . . ." I said, suddenly fighting tears.

It was as if all the pain and hurt I had bottled up came rising to the surface now that I faced the very people who were to blame for it. I began to panic, unable to contain my emotions. I wanted to shout at them, to curse them, to send them to the fate they deserved. But I could not lose control now. I swallowed hard and found my voice. "I just felt my heart moved by the spirit one night, after a visit from my husband," I lied. "The sense of safety and belonging overpowered me and I felt all the fear that had burdened me, relieved."

My tears flowed freely and I knelt before Uncle Kenton, laying my forehead against the floor in a show of complete submission. "I beg your forgiveness, Uncle Kenton, for my betrayal of you and the Brotherhood. I come from five generations of living The Principle, I am a good wife, and I accept my husband's dominion over me in all things. I will defend the faith in word and deed until the day I die!" I sobbed.

The words were a calculated lie to get back into the prophet's good graces. But the pain and the tears were my own.

The room was silent for a moment and I kept my head down, afraid of what might come next. Then I felt Uncle Kenton's hand on my arm, gently leading me to my feet.

"There now, Alva Jane. I know from your tears that your heart is in the right place, that you are truly repentant. Don't cry, little girl. Everything will be fine now," he said, patting my arm and settling me into a chair.

"Get the girl some juice, Sister Maureen," he ordered, and my mother left the room with tears in her eyes.

Uncle Kenton laid a hand on my shoulder and said, "Alva Jane, there is no greater teacher than one who has been to the abyss and come back to the light, no more powerful messenger than one who was lost and now is found. I want you to be the one to talk to other young women in the community who struggle with the requirements of plural marriage. Now and then there are those weak souls who doubt their ability to do what the Lord requires of them. When such a wife is brought to my attention, I want you to speak to her and tell your story."

"Thank you for entrusting me with such a charge, Uncle Kenton."

I was roundly praised by the Priesthood Council, again a member in good standing of the Brotherhood of the Lord. Afterward, I stepped out into the cool night air with my parents and Wade for the walk home.

For the first time in weeks, I felt lightness in my heart. They believed me. They trusted me again. I was one step closer to the moment I would break their trust into a million sharp and bitter pieces.

In the days that followed, word of my repentance spread. Uncle Kenton even spoke of me in the temple, holding me up as an example to all the young women in the community. I was received with open arms and fervent hopes that the prophet was right, that I was a living sign of good fortune again smiling upon the Brotherhood.

But my example alone could not calm the anxiety and paranoia. Construction at the compound gates went into full gear with men working on it around the clock, as if thicker walls and taller turrets could keep out what was threatening us. A few months earlier I would have been like everyone else, hoping and praying for God's favor to smile upon us through the divine prophet. But I knew now that the danger was on the inside. It was in Uncle Kenton's stranglehold of absolute power, and in the blind willingness of the people to be led like sheep to the slaughter.

CHAPTER TWENTY

I WAS HANGING WASH OUT TO DRY ONE CRISP, SUNNY August morning when Jack Norton approached me, coming across the yard with Sister Irene.

"Mr. Norton wants to have a word with you, Alva Jane," Sister Irene said.

"Good morning, Alva. I was hoping you might be able to come over and talk to Brenda? She is struggling with our life here and now that Leigh Ann is pregnant, she has gotten worse. Uncle Kenton suggested that you have a word with her."

Leigh Ann is pregnant?

I knew poor Brenda must be beside herself. I welcomed the chance to talk to her, to see if she might be willing to help me.

"Of course, Brother Jack. I can come tonight if my husband allows it."

He thanked me and left. Sister Irene stood with her arms folded.

"You be careful with that Brenda Norton. She's still working in town, she's got no children. I just don't trust her," she said.

I patted her arm. "As the prophet said, Sister Irene, there is no better messenger than one who has been lost and now is found. I know I can help Brenda to put her heart in the right place."

"Well, I don't like it," Sister Irene grumbled, going back to the house.

I returned to the basket of damp sheets. Brenda drove through the gates of Pineridge every morning. She could come and go as she pleased. If I could just convince her to help me, it would be so easy. I took a frayed pillowcase from the wash line. I would add it to my mending basket, as it would come in handy for carrying the items I would take with me when I escaped.

Everything was falling into place, even this fortuitous invitation to meet with Brenda. I would be leaving soon. I could feel it.

I arrived at Brenda's house early that evening with my scripture books in hand, ready to play the role of the repentant wife preaching the word of salvation. Brenda opened the door and I almost didn't recognize her. She had lost weight and her eyes were listless. Her nails that had once been so pretty and polished were bitten down to the quick. She invited me in and explained that Jack and Leigh Ann were decorating the baby's room upstairs.

"How does it feel having a baby join the family? Is it like you hoped it would be?" I asked.

"Not at all," she whispered. "I just feel so useless and inadequate with Jack doting on her now that the baby's coming. I didn't realize that I would feel this way. . . ."

I knew I didn't have much time to play at this charade. I had to take my chances. "Then why don't you leave? Go back to your parents, go back to your life outside?" I asked.

She looked at me, stunned. "What are you saying?"

I dropped my voice to a whisper. "I have to get out, Brenda. My marriage is a nightmare and I can't take it any longer. I need your help!"

"But what can I do?"

Now I was the one who was stunned. What could she do? Didn't she realize how blessed she was to be able to leave the compound each day, to drive in and out of her own will? "You can leave, Brenda. You have transportation and a life outside. You can take me with you!"

"Oh, no. I can't risk that, Alva. What would happen if they found out?"

I heard Leigh Ann's voice in the hallway. Soon they would be coming down.

Brenda continued, "And I've done something I shouldn't have, Alva. Jack pressured me to open an account for the Brotherhood at the bank, using a phony name so the prophet can run funds through it. It's illegal and if I get caught, I can go to jail. I'm in no position to help anyone, I can't even help myself!"

She began to cry and I wanted to shake her. What had happened to the woman I met that first day? The one who laughed and smiled, who talked about college and hid cans of Coca-Cola in a kitchen cupboard? She wouldn't help me. I had to find another way.

I heard Jack's voice on the stairway and quickly flipped open the Doctrines and Covenants, section 132, and began reading, "'David's wives and concubines were given unto him by me, by the hand of Nathan, my servant, and others of the prophets who had the keys of this power, and in none of these things did he sin against me. . . .'"

The next morning I awoke exhausted, barely able to get out of bed. I wrote it off to having been out to Brenda's the night before but during my kitchen chores I was overcome with a wave of nausea that sent me running to the bathroom. When I returned, Sister Betsy looked at me with a grin.

"How do you feel today, Sister Alva?" she asked, barely able to contain a giggle.

"Not too good. It must be something I ate last night."

"When is your cycle due?" Sister Betsy asked, causing the other sister wives to twitter with laughter—except for Ann Marie.

I felt my insides go cold. My cycle! I hadn't even thought of it. It had come during the first week of my marriage to Wade and it had not come since. I calculated quickly, hoping I had counted the days incorrectly.

"I-I can't be pregnant. . . ." I stammered.

"Oh, yes, you can, if you're fourteen years old with a husband visiting your room every night," Sister Irene said with certainty. "This is just what Wade wanted, to get you with child right away, tame your spirit. Thank the Lord that his prayers were answered!"

Her words made my knees weak. This was what Wade wanted, what they all wanted: to tie me to my husband, to the Brotherhood with a child. I couldn't be pregnant, not with Wade's baby. But in my heart I knew it was true. I had been so busy figuring out how to survive, how to get away, that I hadn't considered that I could be pregnant. My breasts were tender and I was overdue. I had seen my mother and the other sister wives pregnant so many times I could not deny my own symptoms.

I began to cry. What would become of me? How could I escape now, pregnant and alone? And if by some miracle I ever found Joseph John, how could I face him, carrying Wade's baby?

Sister LeNan put a cool washcloth against my head and slid an arm around my shoulders. "Don't be afraid, Sister Alva. The first one is the hardest, after that it gets easier."

I remembered the part I had to play. I knew I couldn't let them see my despair. "I'm just so thankful that the Lord has blessed me so quickly," I said.

Looking around at their faces, my resolve to leave was strengthened. I had to go as soon as possible. I could not let myself be tied to this world by a baby born into the FLDS. But I would not bring my innocent child into it either. If he were a boy, he would not be raised to turn into my father or be expelled like my brother. And if she were a daughter, she would be born free, with a voice to speak her mind and make her life the way she wanted it. For that, I would get out no matter what stood in my way.

CHAPTER TWENTY-ONE

BY THE EVENING, I HAD COME UP WITH A PLAN.
I considered escaping by hiding in one of the construction trucks, but I saw no way to carry Marianne along with me. The only other person I knew who came and went regularly was Brenda Norton. She was unwilling to help me, but that didn't mean that she couldn't. If I could sneak into the trunk of her car, she could drive us out of the compound without ever knowing it.

But hiding in her car meant getting into it and not being seen or heard, with a frightened child in tow. It was a crazy, desperate plan and if we got caught, I didn't want to even imagine what the punishment would be. For me to make another escape attempt and, worse yet, to take the little girl slated to be the prophet's next wife? I knew the price would be blood atonement: the taking of my life to pay for my trespass against the faith. But I couldn't wait any longer; I couldn't take the chance that Marianne could be married to Uncle Kenton any day now. I had my supplies stashed and ready, I had to try to get us out.

The next day I worked extra hard at my chores so that I would be allowed to visit Brenda before dinner. I collected a pile of the prophet's writings on plural marriage and made a great show of my zeal to bring Brenda deeper into the fold, for which I was praised by Sister Irene and Wade.

After supper, I went to the Nortons' house. The garage door was open and I saw Brenda's car parked next to Jack's pickup truck. This was exactly what I had been hoping for. I knocked on the door and found Leigh Ann alone, knitting a baby blanket. She greeted me with a huge, sunny smile, ushering me inside.

She pointed upstairs and whispered, "It's Brenda's night with Jack, but nothing will come of it. She keeps telling him that God will give them a miracle, but soon he's going to have to stop having relations with her if she's barren. Poor thing!"

Leigh Ann settled into the couch and patted the space beside her. "Alva! I'm so happy to see you! I feared you'd be sore at me for telling Jack about your cycle, but I had to, you know."

"Of course, Leigh Ann." She looked so pretty, flush with the glow of pregnancy, content in her life.

"And Mama tells me that you've repented your escape and that now you're happy in your marriage!"

"I couldn't be happier," I lied. "I just wanted to drop off some of Uncle Kenton's writings for Brenda since Jack told me she's struggling with her life here."

Leigh Ann sighed. "She just gets so upset with everything.

I swear, she's as high-strung as a wire coil! She can't get the knack of any home duties, can't sew a lick, and I do all the cooking, what with her going into town every morning. I just can't believe that Jack has allowed her to stay on at the bank."

I thought about the illegal bank account that Jack asked Brenda to open and I knew that he and Uncle Kenton would keep her working there as long as she could be of use to them.

"Poor you! What time does Sister Brenda go in to work?" I asked innocently.

"Oh, quite early since she's got that long drive. She's out the door by six or before. Then Jack goes to oversee the construction so I'm here all alone. I can't wait for the baby to arrive or for Jack to take another wife so I can have some company."

She made chitchat with me about her marriage, how Jack had found a matching bedroom set for her room at the Goodwill in Salt Lake and the dresser even had its own mirror. She was satisfied with so little, she had never imagined anything beyond the walls of Pineridge. I had been like her just a few months ago. She was my sister but I now saw nothing of myself in her.

I had to get into the garage, alone. And I had to do it before Brenda came downstairs and found me there. "Did Brenda ever show you that fancy stitch foot that her sewing machine has?" I asked suddenly, remembering that Brenda's machine and its parts had been in a box stored in the garage.

"No, what can it do?"

"Oh, it does all kinds of fancy buttons and embroidery even! She told me about it when she first moved here."

"Really? She never mentioned it to me."

"Oh, I'm sure she's embarrassed that you sew so well and she can't at all."

Leigh Ann smiled, self-satisfied. "I'd sure like to find it. I could make some pretty baby clothes with it."

"I'll go out and see if it's in the box," I suggested. "Oh, no, Alva, I'll just wait for Brenda to get it," Leigh Ann insisted.

I leaned in to her and whispered, "She might not want to, Leigh Ann. After all, she isn't going to want you to show her up even more than you already do."

Leigh Ann nodded, "You're right; Mama told me the same thing. You go get it, Alva, I'll keep an eye out for them coming downstairs!"

I hurried out to the garage and fished a thin piece of wire I had taken from Wade's toolbox out of my pocket. I popped open the trunk of Brenda's unlocked car. It was roomy enough for me and Marianne to hide in easily and there was even an old blanket folded up in the corner. I secured the trunk door with the wire so that it would stay unlatched and could be opened from the inside, but if no one looked closely, it would appear locked and closed from the outside. I went back to the house.

"I can't find it, Leigh Ann. She's probably got it in her sewing box here in the house. I sure hope she gives it to you; at least you can do something with it!"

Upstairs I heard the bedroom door open and Jack's footsteps in the hallway. "I've got to run, Leigh Ann. Sister Irene will be starting scripture reading at home and I don't want to miss it."

"I'll be sure to give Brenda those pamphlets, Alva Jane. And come back to visit me, soon, okay? I sure miss you!"

I gave her a quick hug and felt a tug in my heart. If all went the way I hoped, she would never see me again.

On the way home, I stopped by Rita Mae's with the pretext of bringing a pressed flower to Marianne. Sister Annie opened the door for me and jerked her head toward the backyard.

"Marianne's out by the shed. Rita Mae punished her for spilling dirty wash water all over the kitchen floor when it had just been polished."

I went out back and found Marianne, who was afraid of the dark, sitting alone behind the toolshed, her big eyes wet with tears. She showed me the red welt on her leg where she had been switched for her clumsiness. I took her little hand in mine and whispered, "How would you like to go to a magic place where there will be no chores and no switches? Do you want to take a magic trip with Auntie Alva?"

Marianne's eyes grew big. "A magic trip?"

"A trip to a faraway place where there's no ironing and no washing, no babies to have their diapers changed."

"No poopy diapers!"

"That's right. Would you like that?"

Marianne nodded.

"Then you have to keep a secret, because if anyone finds out, the magic place will disappear and we won't get to go. When everyone goes to bed tonight, you must come out here and wait for me in this spot. I'll come for you and we'll go together, just you and me."

I knew that coming out here alone would be a lot for her, but it was our only hope.

"Tonight, when everyone goes to sleep. You must come by yourself and tell no one, okay?" I repeated.

She nodded at me but I could see she was frightened. As I hurried home, I prayed that God would give us both the strength to see my plan through.

Before bed, I passed Ann Marie in the hall and tapped my fingers against the back of her hand, our sign that tonight would be the night. I climbed into bed and feigned sleep when Sister Irene closed up the house. Since my repentance, I was no longer locked in my basement room every evening.

I waited until the dead of night when the house was quiet, then slipped my pillowcase of supplies out from the back of the armoire where I had hidden it. I took off my long dress and slid into the slim jeans that Ann Marie had given me. I buttoned up the boy's shirt and tucked my long braid into a knot inside the collar.

I had water and food that I had sneaked out of the pantry, enough to survive a few days in the desert. I had my sewing scissors and knife, the flashlight, and the other items I would need. I was ready. I tiptoed up the stairs of the basement and listened at the doorway. The sounds of the clock ticking in the kitchen carried down the hall. I crept along the main hallway and toward the kitchen where the back door led to the yard and the desert beyond.

As I passed the stairway, I froze in fear. Someone was waiting at the top. I didn't move until I heard the faint *tap-tap* of

Ann Marie's cane. I raised my eyes and saw her silhouette, illuminated only by the thin ribbon of moonlight that spilled across the wood floor. She looked down at me, unable to descend without waking the household. She held her open palm up and I returned the gesture. We were sisters in our suffering and in our shared hopes that I would get out and bring back help.

In the kitchen I left a note telling Sister Irene that I had gone out early to check on my mother who was not feeling well. I knew that would buy me some time while the sister wives attended to their morning chores. If all went well, it would be past nine by the time Sister Irene sent someone to Mama's house to find me.

I glanced up at the thin wooden plaque over the stove that read keep sweet. Not for me, not any longer. I opened the kitchen door and slipped out into the night.

I hurried along the deserted streets of Pineridge, a slim shadow in my disguise. I arrived at Rita Mae's and crept along the fence until I reached the toolshed. I was afraid to look, afraid that Marianne would not be there, or worse yet, that she had told someone of my plan. But when I came around the corner, there she was, alone in her flannel nightdress, her feet in thin tennis shoes, shivering against the night chill.

I bundled her up and quickly changed her into the clothes I had taken from Wade's younger sons. I took her hand and ran with her, past the Brigham tea bushes and the spiny hop sage, past the temple square and the Zion Academy, toward the Norton house.

We approached Brenda's house from the south side, where we could see the windows of the kitchen. The house was dark and mercifully the garage door was still open. We slipped inside and I found the trunk of Brenda's car just as I had left it: secured with wire. I twisted it open and hoisted Marianne inside, all the while whispering in her ear to keep quiet, praying that she wouldn't get scared and cry out.

As I climbed in, a light in the kitchen came on and I gripped the hood of the trunk, holding it almost closed with my fingers. Marianne whimpered and I shushed her. A moment later the garage light came on and Jack Norton came in. I heard him rummaging around in his truck. I prayed that the trunk wouldn't pop open and expose us. He shut off the light and returned to the house. I breathed a sigh of relief, latched the wire, and waited for daybreak, Marianne tucked protectively under my arm.

CHAPTER TWENTY-TWO

I KEPT MARIANNE QUIET UNTIL MORNING WITH whispered tales of how lovely our lives would be in our new home, listening for every sound from the house. I heard activity inside and then Brenda's footsteps in the garage.

Please don't let her find us, I prayed as she walked around the back of the car to climb into the driver's side. She started the engine and pulled out onto the street, winding through Pineridge toward the main gates and the freedom of the highway. There were so many construction trucks that we had to wait at the guard gate while they checked each one. If they looked too closely at Brenda's car, it would all be over for us.

I held my breath, terrified that someone would notice the rigged trunk and discover us. But no one did. Slowly we pulled past the guard gate. I felt the car pick up speed on the open road.

We were outside the compound! Silent tears of relief spilled down my cheeks, but I knew we were far from safe. As soon as our absence was discovered they would be looking for us, fanning out into the desert, into town, with cars and trucks, fueled by my father's fear and the prophet's fury.

We drove for almost an hour before Brenda stopped the car and got out. I waited a few seconds, then pushed up on the trunk and peered out through the crack. We were at a gas station. I realized this must be where Brenda stopped to change into her work clothes each day. I watched her disappear into the restroom attached to the small kiosk where a young clerk was busy talking on a phone. It was time for us to go. I pushed open the trunk and lifted Marianne out, jumping after her. I grabbed my bundle and her hand and we ran into the open desert as fast as we could.

We hid all day and into the night in a cave on the dark side of a red rock formation, more than a mile from the highway. We could not risk traveling by day. It was late when we emerged. The shadows of the desert floor were deep purple, the moon casting a milky white beam illuminating a stand of Utah Juniper and Pinyon Pine trees. I held tight to Marianne's hand as we walked and walked, each step taking us farther away from the Brotherhood of the Lord. I smiled, imagining the faces of Wade, my father, and the prophet when they realized I was gone and had taken Marianne with me. But my joy was tinged by fear. I knew they would not let us go easily.

We ducked beneath a jutting rock ridge just as a summer storm hit. We laughed and held our hands out to catch the falling drops filling up the shallow arroyos with water that would be gone within a day. I cut Marianne's curls close to her head and then took the scissors to my own long braid, cropping it just below my ears. I applied the gooey hair dye and we went into the rain to wash it out, our fair hair now brunette and unrecognizable. We found a small opening in the rock, a crevice really, but big enough for us to hide in. We waited as the sun came up, blazing across the desert as if it too were searching us out as I knew the brotherhood would be. We waited patiently until night fell and it was safe to venture out.

It was almost midnight when we approached the lights of Moab. Marianne was exhausted, hardly able to put one foot in front of the other. We stopped at a service station at the edge of town. In the bathroom, we cleaned up and I fished out the makeup that Ann Marie had given me. With the little brush I applied dark shadow to my eyelids. I rubbed it in and stood back to look at my reflection. With my short dark hair, my smudgy eyes, and the boys' clothes, I looked totally different, both older and tougher than I had imagined. I looked the way I felt inside, having survived and escaped from Pineridge and my life there. The old Alva Jane was gone. This new girl would step out into an alien world and make her own way.

I dragged Marianne along, half-carrying her. I knew firsthand the dangers of going into town, so we hunkered down beside the highway where I could see the headlights of passing cars. We would hitch a ride out of town, as far as anyone was willing to take us. We had to be on our way before morning when it would be too difficult to hide from the search party that I knew Uncle Kenton would have sent to Moab to look for us. As each car approached, I peered out, letting any one with Utah license plates pass us by. I had learned my lesson. I would take no chances on ending up with Mormons who might be sympathetic to the FLDS like Officer Oberg.

I saw an SUV with California plates approach. I stepped out and flagged the car down. It slowed and we ran to the window. A young couple sat inside, the back of the car filled with all kinds of equipment.

"Where are you two going?" the woman asked. She had black hair gathered into a messy ponytail and a colored snake tattoo on her arm. Her nostril was pierced clean through with a silver ring. I had never seen anyone like her before, but I was not in a position to be fussy about who we rode with.

"As far as you'll take us," I said.

"Climb on in, I'll open the back," the young man said. He walked around to the tailgate and lowered it, making room for us. "I'm Mark, this is my girlfriend, Blair. We've been shooting a nature documentary up in the red rocks. We're going back to California," he said, offering me his hand.

"We're headed in that direction too. I'm Brenda," I lied, using the first name that came to mind. "And this is my sister, Leigh Ann."

We climbed into the back of the car and crawled beneath the furniture blankets that Mark gave us for warmth. When we began driving, I saw that Marianne had already fallen asleep. Exhaustion settled over me and I didn't fight it, letting it take me and pull me into the numbness of slumber, safe behind tinted windows as we hurtled along the highway, the lights of Moab receding behind us.

* * *

An hour or so later, we stopped at a Circle K convenience store at the side of the road and Blair turned to me. "You two want anything inside?"

"I have money," I said, jumping out the back of the car to join them. I didn't want to seem like freeloaders taking advantage of their kindness. We left Marianne in a deep sleep in the car.

Inside the store, I wandered the aisles while Blair and Mark used the restroom. The clerk was a skinny, pockmarked man who smoked a cigarette, dropping the ashes into a Styrofoam cup. On the television behind him, I heard a newscaster's voice and I stopped cold in my tracks.

"The police raid this morning on the FLDS community of Pineridge here in the Utah desert has ended with the arrests of Kenton Barton, the self-proclaimed prophet, and his brother, Wade Barton, as well as a score of others. After finding several underage girls pregnant, Children's Services was brought in and many of the youngsters were taken from their homes and put into protective custody. . . ."

The images of Uncle Kenton and Wade, handcuffed and being put into a police car, filled the screen. There had been a raid! How could such a miracle have occurred? Perhaps there truly was a God in heaven who listened to the prayers of those without hope. I thought of Ann Marie, who paid so dearly for her attempt to get away from the misery of her life with Wade. She would be free now. The newscaster moved to talk with a pretty, dark-haired woman in a business suit.

I stood rooted to the spot, unable to tear myself away, my heart pounding wildly.

"This is attorney Lucy Miller, who was instrumental in getting warrants to go into Pineridge. How did that transpire? What tipped you off to the possible abuses that are now being investigated by the authorities?"

Then Mrs. Miller said the words I had not allowed myself to imagine could be true.

"I was contacted by a young man who had been expelled from Pineridge. He was physically assaulted by a group of men and left for dead in the desert. He was told that his fourteen-year-old girlfriend was going to be married against her will to the middle-aged brother of the man who calls himself the prophet of this community, Kenton Barton. We've been hearing about these kinds of cases for years, but as these are closed, insular communities, it is very hard to get a way inside. But this young man showed tremendous courage, giving us names and details of criminal activities that have been taking place as well as other cases of underage girls being forced to marry."

"And where is that young man now?"

"He has since left the state for his own safety. We were hoping to get to Pineridge in time to find the girl he loves, but so far there is no sign of her. We are continuing the search for her."

Joseph John was alive! And he had been trying to help me from the outside, even in my darkest moments when I thought everyone had forsaken me! He had been with me all along. He was out there somewhere, waiting for me. And I would find him.

Then photos of Marianne and me with our fair hair and FLDS clothes flashed on the screen. I flinched and bumped into

Blair and Mark, who had come up behind me, but I had been too engrossed in the news story to notice them.

The newscaster continued, "If anyone has any information on these two missing minors, Alva Jane Merrill and Marianne Ludie Jaynes, please contact the Utah police department."

I looked to Blair and I could see in an instant that she knew we were the missing girls. I didn't want the store clerk to catch on so I moved quickly to the counter with a pack of chewing gum. As Mark paid for their purchases he casually asked the clerk, "So what do you think will happen to those two girls when they find them?"

The clerk snorted. "They'll take 'em back to their parents, where they belong. This is about freedom of religion. Those people should be allowed to practice their faith in peace; they're not hurting anyone. This is Utah, people understand that here. The charges won't stick."

Blair and Mark exchanged a troubled glance but said nothing.

We walked to the car in silence. I climbed in the back wishing we had never stopped, that they had never seen or heard anything of us. Mark closed the door behind me. I heard them talking outside; they were arguing. I pressed my ear to the window to hear what they were saying. Their voices carried and my heart sank.

"We can't just drive away with them, they're minors! We could get into a lot of trouble!" Mark said.

"If two little girls are hiding by the side of the road late at night, they must be getting away from something pretty damn bad! You heard what the clerk said, they'll be sent back to their parents who were trying to marry them off!"

"You don't know that. We're dropping them in Salt Lake City."

I couldn't listen anymore. We had gotten so close to freedom; I could feel it just beyond our reach. Mark and Blair climbed into the front seats, and then Blair turned to me.

"Okay, I figure you are the girls they mentioned in that newscast. If the police are looking for the two of you, we need to know the truth of what is going on."

I saw Mark looking at me in the rearview mirror as he started up the car and began driving. I had to trust them. The road ahead of us was long and the night was deep, silent. I gathered my thoughts for a moment and then I began. I told them my story. I told them everything.

The road disappeared, the car covering mile after mile as my words poured out, filling up the spaces around us in the closed interior. Mark and Blair said nothing.

I saw the road signs for Salt Lake City and I braced myself for what I knew was coming. They would stop to hand us over to the Utah police, and after that, we would be back in the nightmare we had so narrowly escaped, just like the store clerk said.

Mark slowed the car as we approached the turnoff for Salt Lake, then pulled to the side of the highway, the engine idling. He looked at Blair, he looked at me, and then he said, "I think we should drive straight on through to California. What do you think, Alva?"

I stared at them in disbelief.

California. Another world. Another life. Freedom.

"I think that's a very good idea."

Mark stepped on the gas and we pulled back onto the road, disappearing into the inky blackness of the desert night.

AUTHOR'S NOTE

THE FUNDAMENTALIST LATTER DAY SAINTS are a very secretive and insular community, marked by a sense of persecution and being outside the boundaries of general American society. As such, it is quite difficult to access information about their customs and practices, apart from the accounts of members who have abandoned and fled the FLDS. I read many accounts of women who had been raised in the FLDS and subsequently left, and their stories were shockingly similar, from British Columbia to Utah to Arizona to Mexico.

The wording of the sealing ceremonies or marriages described in *Keep Sweet* were drawn from Elissa Wall's courageous book, *Stolen Innocence*, accounting her own forced marriage to her cousin. The words of the character of the prophet, Uncle Kenton, were inspired by transcripts of FLDS texts and sermons. The disciplining of Sister Ann Marie Barton was based upon an account of a woman who witnessed such an event as a girl in an FLDS community. I spoke to a former FLDS member who requested that I do not mention her name or even her initials, given that she still has many relatives living inside the FLDS. I gathered together details and inspiration from all of these stories to weave together Alva's experience in the fictional Pineridge and Brotherhood of the Lord; any similarity to any real or living person is coincidental.

ACKNOWLEDGMENTS

AS WITH any BOOK, THERE IS THE actual WRITING of it and there is the research and preparation as well as the managing of the rest of one's life to find the time and psychological space to write. I have many people to acknowledge in all of those areas. As far as research is concerned, I would like to thank all the courageous women who have left the FLDS and shared their stories, helping to bring awareness to the struggle of young girls who are powerless in these communities. My amazing editor at Simon Pulse, Anica Rissi, had the talent and wisdom to guide me to tell Alva's story in the most moving and effective way. Her input made this book immeasurably better and made me a better writer as well. My book agent, Kevan Lyon, believed in this book, and her support and understanding of this story were instrumental in finding the right home for it. My mother, Dorita, babysat on countless afternoons, making it possible for me to sit behind a closed door in my office and work. Father Mark Weitzel and Elaine Loke allowed me access to the little room at the top of the stairs overlooking the altar, when quiet time and space were impossible to find. I was able to get so much good work done in that blessedly peaceful environment. Thank you to Joseph Sharp, a fellow storyteller, whose miraculous reappearance brought with it support, encouragement, and conversation over coffee, Fight On. And to brave Sadie and Hadji, Fidel and John Moore, who guarded the house and the home fires while I tapped away on a keyboard late into the night.

ABOUT THE AUTHOR

MICHELE DOMINGUEZ GREENE has had a long-standing successful career as an actress, appearing in television, film, and theater. She is active in numerous writing and literacy workshops throughout southern California, and speaks regularly at conferences around the country. She lives with her family in Los Angeles. Find out more at MicheleGreene.com.

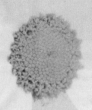

Girls searching for answers . . .
and finding themselves.

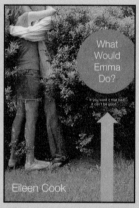

From Simon Pulse | Published by Simon & Schuster